PANDORA
Gets Vain

BOOKS BY CAROLYN HENNESY

Pandora Gets Jealous
Pandora Gets Vain

PANDORA
Gets Vain

CAROLYN HENNESY

BLOOMSBURY
CHILDREN'S
BOOKS

Published by Bloomsbury U.S.A. Children's Books
175 Fifth Avenue, New York, New York 10010

Library of Congress Cataloging-in-Publication Data
available upon request
ISBN-13: 978-1-59990-197-8 • ISBN-10: 1-59990-197-8

First U.S. Edition 2008
Typeset by Westchester Book Composition
Printed in the U.S.A. by Quebecor World Fairfield
2 4 6 8 10 9 7 5 3 1

All papers used by Bloomsbury U.S.A. are natural, recyclable products
made from wood grown in well-managed forests. The manufacturing processes
conform to the environmental regulations of the country of origin.

For Donald

INTA QALBI

For Donald

INTA QALBI

PANDORA
Gets Vain

CHAPTER ONE

Storm

7:56 p.m.

A storm such as Pandy had never seen hit three days after they reached the open sea. The waves were as tall as temple pillars and the winds were shredding holes in the enormous black-and-white striped mainsail. Hard rain was pouring from the sky with the ferocity of a waterfall, and the ship had been careening, skidding, and lurching violently ever since it had passed the jagged outcropping of rock that formed the coastline of western Greece, just past the city of Methone.

Almost an hour earlier, as the first gusts of wind began to swirl about the ship, the captain insisted that his passengers go below deck immediately. Pandy and her friends, Alcie and Iole, had come up topside for a breath of fresh air only moments before. They tried to comply with the captain's orders, but as they took their first steps from the bow toward the small set of stairs at the stern, the winds immediately shifted, slapping them back against the railings and almost blowing them into the water. For the last forty-five minutes, the hurricane had pinned all three girls and several well-seasoned sailors to the railings, the huge mast, and the cargo crates that were tied down to the deck. The black clouds made it difficult for Pandy to keep her friends in sight. She knew Alcie would be able to hold on; in fact, Alcie's recent affliction of having two left feet had somehow made her able to negotiate her way around the ship. Instead of constantly veering off to her right as she did on land, the gentle glide of the hull over the water had miraculously straightened out Alcie's stride and before the storm had descended, Alcie was seriously considering becoming a sailor. Now, Pandy could just make out Alcie against the mast, her hands intertwined in the sail ropes, riding out the storm like it was merely a light breeze.

Iole was a much different story, and it was only when the first bolts of lightning began striking the water all around them that Pandy saw her little friend was in serious trouble. Iole had been thrown against the railings easily with the first gust. Now her thin arms and legs were slipping through the large gaps between the railing posts. The rain, the constant spray of seawater, and the dip of the ship as it crested wave after wave was making it impossible for Iole to hang on. She couldn't keep a grip on the railing posts; they were too thick and the wood was gummy and slimy from years of exposure to the salty sea air.

Pandy's place on the deck was precarious enough; she was being tossed about between two large packing crates, and she could feel her shoulders and legs beginning to bruise. But she'd wrapped her arms around the ropes that held the crates to the deck and she felt that, though she was going to be black and blue, she was fairly safe. Now, however, with lightning illuminating Iole almost half overboard, Pandy knew that if she didn't get to Iole fast, she'd be less one best friend.

Pandy freed her arms from the ropes and crept forward on her hands and knees over the slippery deck toward Alcie and the mast. Alcie's body was turned in such a way that she didn't yet see Iole was in trouble. Pandy screamed at the top of her lungs, pointing toward the railing. Alcie squirmed around the mast to look and shrieked, sticking one of her left feet out for Pandy to grab hold of. Pandy pulled herself over Alcie's leg, inching her way up to a standing position, and began trying to untie the heavy rope coiled around the mast.

"What are you doing?" yelled Alcie.

"I'm gonna try to get this to Iole!" Pandy yelled back.

Suddenly a rough hand yanked the end of the rope out of her grasp and grabbed her forearm.

"That rope holds the mainsail! You could bring down the whole ship, you fool!" said one of two sailors who'd also been pinned against the mast by the winds.

"My friend is going to be killed!" Pandy screamed, pointing to the railing.

"Too bad for her," yelled the other sailor, lightning flashing on his grimy, toothless face. "But you're not going to wreck the *Peacock!*"

"What?" gasped Pandy, taking in a mouthful of salt water. "What did you say?"

"The *Peacock* has weathered worse than this and you stupid maidens are not going to do anything to destroy her," snarled the first sailor, his hand still clapped around Pandy's.

"Great Gods," Pandy thought, "that's it!" The name of the ship was the *Peacock* and that could mean only one thing. *One thing!*

Hera, the Queen of Heaven, whose primary symbol was the peacock, had sent this storm. Pandy was never more sure of anything in her life. Hera had somehow seen to it that Pandy and her friends had boarded this ship, and now she was bent on sending it to the bottom of the sea. Why oh why had she not recognized the danger before they got onboard? Had she even noticed the name of the ship?

At that moment, the *Peacock* fell into a deep trough in the waves and the sailor released his grasp on

Pandy's arm to brace himself against the mast. Pandy went tumbling—flying was more like it—toward Iole and the railing. She hit the railing so hard that she thought she'd cracked a rib. She was about to be tossed to the other side of the ship when she saw Iole's hand just inches away. Instantly she grabbed on to it, and the force of the lurch and Pandy's extra weight helped drag Iole back on board a bit. But there was nothing else to hold on to, nothing to tie them down. The packing crates were too far away. Alcie had attempted Pandy's idea of using the mast rope, but she was now pinned by the two sailors, who kept her restrained even though she was trying to bite them.

Iole looked at Pandy, unable to speak, her eyes red from crying and salt water.

"I need a rope," Pandy thought, now completely desperate. "All I need is a stupid *rope*!"

The following instant, a flash of lightning carved the face of the great goddess Athena in the air precisely in front of Pandy's nose. Athena looked directly at Pandy and winked at her.

And then Pandy had an idea.

Only a week before, Athena had given Pandy a magic rope, one that would grow longer or shorter, thicker or thinner, depending on what was needed. All Pandy had to do was ask the rope to do something and the next moment it was done. But each time she'd used it before, the rope had actually been in her hands. Now the rope was coiled securely inside her leather carrying pouch, which was stowed in her cabin safely below deck.

There was no way she could physically get to it, not without letting go of Iole, and Pandy knew she'd never make it below deck and back in time.

But Athena had not appeared to her just to give her a wink.

"Rope . . . come to me . . . ," Pandy began to mutter under her breath.

"Rope . . . come to me . . . *now!*" She said the words again and again, without the faintest notion if her summoning was working.

As the *Peacock* rode up another crest, Pandy and Iole were almost vertical to the deck. Only Iole's foot, hooked around one of the railing posts, and Pandy's left arm, hooked around another post, kept them from falling down toward the stern of the ship.

"Rope . . . come to me . . . I need you . . . now!" Pandy said again and again.

The ship plunged down into the trough and Pandy lost her grip on Iole's wrist as Iole, screaming, slipped halfway through the railing.

As Pandy was thrown upside down with the force of the plummet, a bolt of lightning struck close to the passageway opening. Pandy's head jerked toward the flash and her eye caught sight of something thin and silvery on deck. The magic rope was snaking its way toward her from the passageway opening. The sailors trapped on deck didn't even notice; they were too busy trying to save their own lives.

"Faster!" she cried. Instantly the rope was in her hands.

"Longer . . . thicker!" she yelled and the rope obeyed.

Iole screamed again. At least Pandy thought it was Iole. It might have been the giant peacock that had appeared suddenly, hovering in the air for an instant over her head, a brilliant sapphire blue and ruby red bird, screeching at the top of its voice.

Iole was almost gone, only her feet, hooked to two of the railing posts, were still visible.

"Catch Iole now!" Pandy yelled. One end of the rope flew from Pandy's hands and disappeared overboard.

"Bring her back!" Pandy cried, not knowing if the rope could even understand more complex commands. But the next moment Iole was on deck, the rope wound about her waist and shoulders in a beautiful little harness.

"Hold us both to the railing!" Pandy said, and the rope stretched itself to be able to firmly secure both Pandy and Iole to the posts, and wrapped itself around the two girls with a series of intricate knots.

In that instant, Pandy realized that if the ship held together they would all be safe.

Then the storm stopped. Completely.

Within minutes, the sky was clear and blue. The coastline of Greece was visible once again and the jagged rock formations were in exactly the same spot as before the storm. Which, Pandy knew, meant that the *Peacock* hadn't moved at all. The Ionian Sea lay before them smooth as a looking glass.

"Rope . . . let us go," Pandy said softly. The rope released her and Iole instantly. "Smaller . . . very small," she said, and the rope nestled itself into the palm of her hand. She tucked it behind her silver girdle.

The sailors began to crawl from their hiding places all over the deck. The two who had restrained Alcie immediately backed away, because she was still nipping at them.

"Come on, Iole," Pandy said, helping her waterlogged friend to her feet. They stumbled over to Alcie, standing against the mast, her hands still intertwined with the ropes. Alcie was swearing at the sailors who'd held her captive, demonstrating her other affliction: anytime she cursed (which was a lot), it came out as . . . fruit.

"Figs! Lemons! Pears to you both!" she called to the now-laughing sailors, her arms over her head.

"Alcie . . . you can let go now, you know," Pandy said.

"Oh!" Alcie said with a start. "Oh, right!"

The three girls dragged themselves past the crew members now checking the ship, the deck, and the cargo for damage. The men were calling out that the storm was bad all right but they'd seen worse, each one trying to outdo the others with tall tales, as the girls slipped down into the passageway below deck.

Safe and warm once again, the girls locked their cabin door and took off their soaked outer togas, hanging them on the ends of their sleeping cots to dry. No one spoke for a long time.

"What was that?" Iole said finally.

"Duh!" said Alcie, sitting on her cot with her back against the hull of the ship. "Only the worst storm *I've* ever seen."

"It was more than that," said Iole, turning to Pandy, "wasn't it?"

"I don't know. I-I think . . . ," Pandy stammered. "Yes. It was more than just a bad storm."

"What? What do you mean more?" Alcie asked.

"Pandy . . . I saw the peacock in the air," Iole said.

"What peacock?" said Alcie.

"If the peacock had tried to help in some way, or calm the winds," Iole went on, "but it was screeching . . ."

"I know . . . it's a sign of some sort," Pandy replied.

"Sign? What sign?" Alcie barked.

"Alcie, just listen, okay?" said Pandy, curling her legs up underneath her and rubbing her side where she'd smashed into the railing. Dido, her dog, had been severely tossed about in their cabin during the storm and now he laid his head, a small cut just above his right eye, in Pandy's lap. "If I knew exactly what was going on, believe me, I'd tell you. I know you guys didn't have to come with me on this quest, and you know I'd never keep anything from you."

She dropped her voice to a whisper.

"Hera sent the storm. I'd bet all our food supplies on it. Did you see how quickly the storm cleared up once there was no chance that Iole or I would be killed?"

"But why, Pandy?" said Iole. "She's the one who gave you the map when you were up on Olympus in front of Zeus. She's the one who took pity on you and convinced Zeus not to boil you in oil, but to let you come on this search. She gave you the gold coins as a clue to go to Egypt."

"Look," Pandy sighed, "all I know is that Hera says one thing and means another. And she doesn't like me; she pretends to, but she doesn't. At all."

She put the small coil of rope back in her leather carrying pouch.

"Why wouldn't she like you?" asked Alcie.

"I don't know yet," Pandy shot back, then she dropped her voice again. "The only thing I'm pretty sure of is that whatever she's doing . . . it's going to get worse."

CHAPTER TWO

On Board

7:09 a.m.

The following morning, Pandy forced herself back onto the top deck. Now, standing at the railing, the old wood still soaked through, Pandy kept looking back. The coast of mainland Greece had disappeared at least twenty minutes ago, but she was still stubbornly staring behind her, trying to will it back into view.

The large cargo ship carrying Pandora Atheneus Andromaeche Helena, her best friends Alcie and Iole, and her white shepherd dog, Dido, had left the port city of Crisa four days earlier heading for Egypt. The girls had wanted to book a cabin on a passenger ship, something a bit more comfortable, but none were leaving for Alexandria for at least a week and there was no time to spare. They also didn't have the money for comfort so they had to make do with a freight ship laden with crates of Greek tiles, baskets of cured meat, sacks of falafel mix, and a gift from the University of Athens of hundreds of leather-bound books for the magnificent library at Alexandria. It had taken the oarsmen the better part of a day to move the heavy ship through the Gulf of Corinth, negotiate a narrow straight, and sail out into the open Ionian Sea on their way across the Mediterranean.

Pandy had stood on deck almost the entire time. Long before Alcie and Iole had awakened each morning and long after they went below deck to their closet-sized cabin each night, Pandy was at the railing, watching as Greece floated by and wondering when, if ever, any of them would set foot on its shores again.

Almost three weeks had gone by since she'd seen her family or her home in Athens. And what weeks they had been. Never before, she thought, in the long history of the world, had one person caused so much trouble. Just by being dumb . . . and selfish . . . and totally irresponsible. Even though she was thirteen and officially a maiden and supposed to know better.

It had been almost six weeks since she had taken the box containing all the evils that could plague mankind to school for a big class assignment—just to show off. Her father, Prometheus, had been entrusted by Zeus himself with keeping the box safe and sealed. Prometheus made Pandy promise that she would never, ever, ever touch it. She had given her word to him when she was six years old. And seven years later, just to be better than everyone else, she had totally and completely disobeyed him. All for a stupid school project! The box had accidentally been opened and everything had escaped.

Well, that was the way her pathetic life went—duh! No surprise.

Pandy was even sorry that the two meanest girls at the Athena Maiden Middle School, Helen and Hippia, had been reduced to big hairless salamanders because they had been standing too close to the box when the lid flipped up. Okay, it was kinda, sorta their fault: they *had* tricked Pandy into letting them see the box and they *had* promised they wouldn't open it and it *was* kinda nice that they were out of her life and weren't tormenting her and her friends anymore, but no one deserved to be turned into a flopping black lizard.

The small island of Cythera at the southern end of Greece was now fading from view. What kind of people lived there, she wondered. How had they been affected by all the trouble that was now loose in the world? What had she done to them?

Pandy suddenly wanted to fly overboard and into the ocean. Even having been nearly drowned only the day before, she wanted to swim to the island and stay there, hiding among the rocks and cypress trees, eating nothing but berries and green olives ... maybe a rat. She *should* eat a rat. A big rat the size of a goat.

She didn't want to go to Egypt. She didn't want to fulfill her promise to Zeus to recapture, within six months' time, every evil plague that had escaped, no matter where it was, no matter how dangerous. She just wanted to hide and slowly waste away on that island right out there; her bones poking through her skin, her nails becoming claws, and her eyeballs falling into the dirt as she died—finally—of starvation.

Then Pandy remembered Zeus's words to her as she had stood before him and all the other immortals weeks earlier in the great hall on Mount Olympus: "I would follow you, Daughter of Prometheus. I would follow you down to the depths of your dreams . . . I would hunt you into the flames of Tartarus and bring your body back for the punishment you deserve."

And she had known even then that Zeus, Supreme Ruler and King of all Gods, would keep his word. After the box had been opened, Pandy and her family were summoned to Mount Olympus, where she had been given a choice. She alone of the great house of Prometheus would recapture the evils or her family would suffer unspeakable torments for the rest of eternity. If she didn't accept or if she failed in her quest, everyone related to her would be cleaning sewage pits in the underworld (and that would be the fun part) forever.

"Okay," Pandy thought. "So jumping overboard is out."

Perhaps the whole ordeal wouldn't be so terrible. After all, they had already managed to capture one of the seven most deadly plagues. Just days earlier, in Delphi, they had trapped Jealousy. The girls had been attacked by Harpies and Iole had almost been roasted to death over the sacrificial fire, but in the end they had been successful, and now they were on their way to Egypt to capture Vanity. And they had just managed to weather what was probably the worst storm in the entire history of the planet. So, how bad could it be? Of course, neither she nor Alcie nor Iole spoke Egyptian and she had no idea where to look for Vanity if they ever actually got there . . . but how bad could it be?

Really?

"Sheesh," she thought. They were all toast.

There was only one good thing that had come from any of this: she had discovered her power over fire. Well . . . she'd discovered that she had a power over fire; she didn't know exactly how extensive it was or all the things that she could do with it. But it went way beyond the little trick her father taught her of creating heat with her breath by blowing on embers or wood or coals and heating them until they glowed red hot.

Turning forward, she saw a larger island coming into view. She stopped one of the sailors and asked what it was.

"Crete," he replied tersely, and went about his task of tying off the freshly patched mainsail. None of the sailors had been very nice to the girls during the voyage. They weren't mean exactly, they were just busy, and Pandy and Iole tried to keep out of their way. Alcie, however, couldn't have cared less about being underfoot and was fascinated by shipboard life.

Hearing the name of the island, Pandy immediately went down below to the small cabin she shared with her friends. Dido was asleep on Pandy's cot, but Alcie and Iole were nowhere to be found.

She walked the short passageway to the oar room. Peeking her head in, she saw two hundred men—slaves, actually—sitting on long benches, twenty rows deep. An aisle that ran the length of the room (which almost ran the length of the ship) cut the rows in half: five men on one side, five on the other. Each group of five held fast to a large oar that stuck out of a little hole in the side of the ship and down into the water. The men were pulling these heavy oars back and forth. It was one sailor's job to pound the drum at the far end of the room so the oars were moved in perfect unison and didn't get smashed together. Another man, the leader of the rowers, walked up and down the aisle calling time with the drummer.

"Stroke! Stroke! Stroke!" he called endlessly.

Pandy saw Alcie where she usually found her friend these days: sitting by the drummer, mesmerized as he beat out the rhythm. She caught Alcie's eye and motioned for her to come. Alcie skirted the caller, ignoring his dirty look as she walked straight as an arrow up the aisle.

"This better be good," Alcie griped. "I'm having fun and you had to interrupt. Oranges!"

Alcie and Iole had also been standing close to the box when it had first been opened. Not as close as Helen and Hippia, so they were still fairly functional and had all their hair, but both of Pandy's friends had been affected. Iole came down with a nasty case of wiggling, tickling bumps on her arms and legs, but her skin had been healed when she was suspended over the sacrificial flame of the Oracle at Delphi. Unfortunately, Alcie's afflictions were still very much there.

"Come on," said Pandy. "We've got to find Iole."

"Why?"

"You'll see."

Pandy led Alcie down another passageway. They passed the crew quarters and the small, empty dining hall. They passed the sleeping quarters for the captain of the ship, which also served as the chart room and library. At last they came to the galley. This was where Iole could be found much of the time, in a small anteroom; petting the lamb, the goat, the three piglets, and the two chickens that were going to be used to feed the crew and the four passengers. To satisfy over two hundred people during a voyage lasting a week and a half, the cook was in the habit of creating giant cauldrons of stew and using lots of vegetables to extend such meager amounts of meat. But Iole had made it her mission to try to get the cook to go completely vegetarian. At first the cook paid no attention to her because she was small and fragile; not even a maiden yet, still just a girl. But when Iole continued to show up at the galley entrance, he threatened to roast her instead of the goat.

"I've been roasted by the best," she said. "Your little fire doesn't scare me."

The cook, whose long nose gave him a somewhat rodentlike appearance, screwed up his face and chased her out into the passageway. But she kept coming back. Finally, partly out of respect for the fact that she was a paying passenger but mostly because she reminded him of his daughter back in Greece, he allowed her to sit in the corner and try to convince him exactly why he should spare the animals. She'd done a good job for the first three days, and together they created some wonderful things with chickpeas and lentils. But just this morning, Iole had awoken to the smell of . . . goat smoke. After racing down the passageway, she had stood teary eyed at the galley entrance. The cook looked up at her in the doorway. At first he tried to bluff and joke his way out from under her gaze, but then he became angry.

"It's my job, Iole!" he said.

Iole said nothing in return. Finally, the cook just broke down and cried.

"I'm sorry, honey. But I'm running out of ideas and after battling the storm yesterday, the crew wants meat!"

When Pandy and Alcie came into the galley, they found Iole and the cook sitting at the table. He was staring off into space, twitching slightly, and she was writing her mother's rice recipes on sheets of papyrus, every so often patting his trembling hand.

"Iole, you need to see this," Pandy said.

"What?" asked Iole.

"Come on. It's a surprise," said Pandy.

"Figs! She won't tell me either," said Alcie.

The three girls left the cook, and Pandy led the way toward the stairs.

"I don't want to go back up there!" Iole said. "In fact, after that storm, I intend to remain below deck for the rest of the voyage, thanks very much."

"Just trust me, okay?" said Pandy, forcing Iole ahead of her up the stairs and onto the deck.

"Look!" said Pandy, pointing to the island, now coming clearly into view.

"Oh! Oh!" exclaimed Iole, rushing to the railing she'd nearly slipped through the day before.

"I was pretty sure you'd want to see it," Pandy said.

"What?" said Alcie. "It's an island. The sea is full of 'em!"

"Oh, Pandy . . . ," Iole sighed.

"Okay . . . yet another thing that I'm so totally left out of," said Alcie.

"I'm sorry, Alcie," said Iole, turning to her. "But that's Crete. That's my home."

"It's been over five years. How do you know?" asked Alcie.

There was a long pause.

"I'd know it in my sleep," Iole said softly.

She paused again, leaning forward into the railing, her eyes searching the distance.

"There's the small point where my dad used to take the family on day trips—picnics and things. Just beyond that is a little bay, and after that is the forest where my grandmother is buried."

"Where's your grandfather?" asked Alcie.

"He's a rock."

Pandy and Alcie whipped their heads around in unison to look at Iole.

"Hades turned him into a rock because he swore once and used Hades' name. Apparently it was really,

really terrible. Something like how he didn't believe in the underworld, and even if he did, when he died he wasn't going to pay Charon to ferry him across the river Styx. Mom says he yelled about having to pay so much in taxes when he was alive, that he wasn't going to pay anything else when he was dead. So Hades said something like, 'Fine, then you just won't go.' And turned him into a boulder. Mom and Dad kept him in the courtyard at first. But when Grandma died, they used him to mark her gravesite. So, in an obtuse way, they're together."

Pandy and Alcie had absolutely nothing to say. But the two of them couldn't help but think of every time they had mentioned the gods' names in vain.

The three girls remained at the railing, watching as the ship sped past the western tip of Crete. Suddenly, they heard a loud thud far across the deck, inside the passageway entrance. Turning around, they saw a large head covered in blond curls poke out into the sunlight.

"Oh no," said Pandy.

"Oh my," said Iole.

"Oh yes-s-s!" said Alcie.

"How does he *always* know where we are?" Pandy said, the three girls turning their faces back out to sea.

"It's not that big of a ship, Pandy. There aren't that many places to hide," Iole replied.

"Who wants to hide anyway?" said Alcie, now

sporting a wide grin . . . which on Alcie was slightly terrifying.

"Tell me again why he has to be here?" said Iole.

"I've told you a hundred million times. I told you right after it happened back in Crisa. The man who booked our passage to Egypt wouldn't sell me the tickets unless his son came with us. As protection. The man didn't think that three girls traveling alone was very wise," Pandy said.

"Smart man. So totally smart," said Alcie, watching the blond head, now attached to a large, well-muscled body, searching for the three girls.

"And you didn't tell him that Dido was protection enough?" asked Iole.

"I did. He thought that was very funny," said Pandy. "He said he just wouldn't feel right; that since he could only get us onto a cargo ship, if anything happened, he'd feel responsible. That's why his son would be the perfect choice. He's young, he's strong . . ."

"He's completely cute," said Alcie.

". . . and his dad wants him in the family export business so he needs to get used to being on a ship," Pandy summed up. "He's not that bad. And he's stopped sleeping outside our cabin door, so at least we're not tripping over him anymore."

The blond-headed body was now lumbering up to the three girls.

"Here he comes," said Iole, quietly, as a large shadow blocked the sun.

Pandy and Iole slumped. Alcie straightened up.

"Hi, Homer," said Alcie brightly.

CHAPTER THREE

Homer

7:58 a.m.

"Uh . . . hi," said a gruff voice as they stood at the railing, Crete now fading into the distance.

They turned and craned their necks upward to stare at the blond-haired, blue-eyed, six-foot-two wall of muscle who was, for the duration of the voyage, their protector.

Pandy's thoughts flashed to the first time she'd seen Homer, only a few days earlier. Entering the shipping agency back in Crisa to inquire about cabin rates, she'd found the red-faced proprietor yelling at Homer, who was almost on the verge of tears.

"You *will* go to Alexandria and you *will* deliver these parcels to your uncle and I will hear no more about it!" yelled the older man, his loose brown teeth knocking and clattering in his mouth as he spoke.

"But Dad," said Homer. "I just came back from Ethiopia!"

"And why did you come back? Because you couldn't hack it in gladiator school! So you dropped out. I scrimp and save for years but you 'don't like it' in the arena. At sixteen you think *you* know what's best, so you just quit!"

"I didn't want to go in the first place," said Homer.

"Oh, that's right," his father spat. "My son wants to be a *poet*! Well too bad. You'll learn the family business and like it!"

Pandy had almost coughed up a lung as she exclaimed loudly, "Ex-*cuse* me!"

Both men had turned, seeing her for the first time.

"I'm sorry to interrupt," she said, "but I'd like to ask . . . um . . . inquire about going to Egypt. Alexandria, actually. How much would it cost to get there? Me and two other people? And my dog?"

The older man's eyebrows had stood almost on end, seeing a young maiden alone in his offices. Before he would book her passage, Pandy had to answer many questions about where she was from, why she was traveling without her parents, and who was traveling with her. She told only one or two teeny little fibs: traveling with her sisters, tragic death in the family, etc.

"Fine," the man had said at length. "I have a ship leaving tomorrow. It's a cargo ship, so you'll be cramped, but you'll get there. And Homer is going, so he can look out for you."

"Homer is not going!" said the boy.

"Homer *is* going," said the man, turning to his son, "if I have to plant the toe of my sandal where Apollo doesn't shine! You're still not too big, my boy . . . Well, yes you are, but I don't care. You'll deliver the parcels, have a nice chat with your uncle about the import/export business, *and* watch over this lovely maiden and her sisters on the way. Period!"

Pandy had felt herself blush at being called lovely. The man tallied up the charge and wrote out the tickets and a letter of introduction for the captain of the ship. Pandy paid for the passage. As she left, she'd wondered if she'd actually see Homer aboard the ship and whether or not he'd be manacled. The three girls had spent the night in a small inn, listening to Pandy's experience in procuring the tickets and then creating a fake history for themselves as they were all "sisters" now.

The next morning, Homer and his father were standing on the appointed dock. The older man had looked strangely at Alcie and Iole, noticing almost nothing but differences among the girls. Pandy smiled weakly, Iole kept her head down, and Alcie was supposed to do the same. But after one glance at Homer, Alcie had decided that the view was better if she looked up.

Homer said nothing. He didn't even acknowledge the girls and he pretended not to notice when Dido licked his hand.

The first day out, as the captain carefully negotiated the straits between the Gulf of Corinth and the Ionian Sea, Iole caught Homer as he went up on deck for fresh air and tried to talk to him. But he didn't even grunt at her and Iole decided he was plainly "simple." Alcie found him at the railing as she marched from mast to mast, loving the way the sea made her walk straight.

"Hi," she said sweetly.

"Whatever," he said, moping his way back below deck.

"I so totally agree!" she called after him. "You know it!"

Now, on this fourth day, he stood blocking the sun.

"So, Homer," Alcie said, a softer quality to her voice that made Pandy and Iole turn and stare at her with wonder, "how'd you make out during the storm yesterday? Pretty wild, huh?"

Pandy and Iole looked at Alcie like she'd suddenly grown a second head.

"Um . . . I was asleep," Homer replied.

"Why does that not surprise me?" Iole said under her breath, turning back to look at Crete.

Homer was almost always in his room. Except for the first night, when he'd camped outside the girls' door on his father's orders. The girls had spent most of the night talking about their quest, not realizing he was there, until he fell asleep and crashed his head into the cabin door as he hit the floor.

They managed to convince him that, with a heavy bolt on their door, he was free to stay in his own cabin. The girls had been a bit concerned about what Homer might have overhead, but he'd given no indication that *anything* was going on inside his head, much less an interest in their quest.

"Oooh, sleeping! Well, that's fun too, I suppose." Alcie giggled and choked on her tongue.

"Pandy," said Homer, totally ignoring Alcie, who now actually was turning purple from choking, "my father wanted me to, like, every once in a while, see if you guys were okay and . . . stuff. So . . . after that storm . . . like, are you guys okay?"

"Um . . . we're okay, Homer," said Pandy, lightly patting Alcie's back. "Thanks for . . . um . . . everything."

"Yes," said Iole icily, "thanks for the timely concern."

"Cool. So . . . um . . . that time I was outside your cabin, I kinda heard why you guys—I mean, maidens—are really going to Alexandria and about the gods and stuff. And Pandy, I just wanted to say that those girls who opened the box are very uncool. So I won't tell my dad you lied. Okay . . . like . . . good luck saving the world. And maybe I'll see you guys—I mean, maidens—later, y'know, around Egypt."

As he walked away, Iole and Pandy turned to look at each other, horrified at having been overheard, but Alcie just stared at the spot where Homer had stood.

"Great hulking pomegranates!" she yelled, finally clearing her throat. "When we get ashore, he's just gonna leave us!"

CHAPTER FOUR

Aeolus

11:02 a.m.

Compared to the magnificent palace up on Mount Olympus, the earthly home of Aeolus, King of the Winds, was puny and insignificant. It was a floating island with no name that drifted with the ocean currents, traveling all of earth's waterways. Aeolus himself rarely knew where he would wake each day, swirling in amongst icebergs and frozen rocks or passing by islands full of date palms. Yet his island was still almost ten square miles in area and, as Aeolus allowed Notus, the South Wind, freedom to blow lightly at all times, the air was always fresh and the open rooms always swept clean. Small birds that could not scale the heights of Olympus fluttered and played on the warm breeze. Plants, flowers, and trees bent and swayed joyfully, creating ever-changing tapestries of light and shadow. Elaborate sets of wind chimes were placed around the gardens and throughout the house so the tinkling of glass beads, gold cylinders, or wooden pipes delighted the ear with music.

One of only a few immortals to actually live on earth, Aeolus, at any time, could also command Notus to blow in any desired scent, filling the house with whatever fragrance he wished: roses from the gardens of Moab, honeysuckle from Damascus, salty drops off the Black Sea, or the pungent smells of Syrian cooking spices.

Hera, however, was completely oblivious to these earthly delights. She had summoned Aeolus to his workroom at the tip of the island very, very early that morning. When he had entered, she was silhouetted against the huge panes of glass that formed one wall, allowing a view of whatever lands the island was passing. She hovered in the air just off the floor, her eyes trained on him like a falcon's. His fear didn't register clearly because the skin on Aeolus's face was always pulled back tightly, as if he were in the path of a hurricane, but his body was shaking badly. He had stood silently, quivering for several minutes, before she finally descended and began yelling.

Now she paced about his workroom with angry, lumbering steps. Aeolus ran after her frantically, righting jars of winds, catching pots of gusts and gales, and steadying mixing bowls that were bumped and jostled as she passed by table after table.

"You call that a storm?" she screamed, turning

suddenly, the sleeve of her brilliant blue robe knocking over a jar labeled WINDS OF CHANGE. "I specifically came to you for a bone-cracking, boat-breaking, lungs-filled-with-water, sink-to-the-bottom *storm!* One that would send those girls tumbling into the sea! You're the silly King of Winds, for my sake! You're supposed to know which winds to mix together to produce the right effect. But I could have done better simply by exhaling!"

"That would kill us all," muttered Aeolus very quietly under his breath, fixing the lid on the jar she'd almost spilled.

"Sorry? Didn't quite catch that. Did you say something?" barked Hera, crossing to him with one large stride.

"I said, gracious Queen of Heaven," he recovered quickly, "that it was still a squall. I did try my best, my lady. And it should have worked."

"It didn't!" said Hera. "So before I have you tied to the Sirens' rock and let their singing drive you mad for eternity, what else do you have for me?"

She forced a smile onto her face as if to say "How hard can it be? I'm *so* easy to please!" Opening her arms wide as she looked about the room, she sent a large clay pot crashing to the floor.

"Ahh!" cried Aeolus, withering slightly.

"Oops. Sorry . . . was it important?"

"No. No." Aeolus fought to keep himself from

collapsing with rage and sorrow. "Just a rare wind from Carthage. One that brings the scent of war. Almost extinct. In a one-of-a-kind pot about three thousand years old. But no—no biggie."

"Good. So . . . what else?"

"Well, of course, great one . . . of course I'll formulate just the right thing for your needs," Aeolus said. "But unless these old eardrums have been permanently wind damaged, you did say you didn't necessarily want the girls killed, right?"

"Killed? No . . . it's not time yet. Someone in a position of power on Olympus—who shall remain nameless but is my husband—would become extremely suspicious and spoil all the fun I'm having. So, killed? No. But I expected you to at least get them into the water! Then I could send a few flesh-eating sea creatures to mangle them a bit. Make it look like an accident, that sort of thing. That's what I want! Go ahead, get to work. I'll just wait here."

She plopped into his favorite chair, the one he always sat in to create his wind recipes; the one that he'd sat on for centuries, which curved so comfortably to his bottom.

Aeolus spun on his heels and furtively surveyed his huge workroom. Jars upon jars, a few older ones of clay and porcelain, but most of clear glass, lined the shelves along the walls, stretching from the floor to the ceiling some twenty meters high. There were thousands of them, each labeled with the type of wind or gust inside, where it came from, and what its best uses were.

Blowa-Blowa (medium strength), from the region south of the great Sahara Desert, good for shaking spiders and snakes from the tops of trees.

Northeasterly Winds (strong), off of the great ocean that lay to the west of the Mediterranean, excellent for driving ships miles off course.

Coif Cruncher (strong), from the icy lands to the north, best used for ruining women's perfectly styled hairdos (for special occasions) in one cold blast.

Whizzer (medium), a short, sharp burst of hot air out of Syria; used to blow reams of important papyrus papers out of the hands of politicians as they left the government houses.

Somna-Gust (mild), from the Dead Sea, often used by Morpheus in combination with Baby-Lamb's Breath when cranky children refuse to go to sleep.

He had them all cross-referenced and categorized.

One whole wall was filled with containers of winds to be mixed only with various rains: Helter-Pelter, Wet Wash, and the furious Toga-Soak—a wet wind so powerful it could waterlog a person's undergarments in mere seconds.

Another large section contained winds and gales to be used only at sea: Mast-Snapper, Scent of Land, and the inescapable Maelstrom, the wind Aeolus used to create deadly whirlpools.

A row of jars sitting on the bottom shelf housed winds specifically designed for natural disasters, such as the Volcanic Ash Carrier and Boulder Assist, to help move rocks and stones a little farther during earthquakes and landslides.

And a smaller section still was the single shelf, high in a back corner, where Aeolus kept the subtle and delicate indoor winds: Whisper Breath, Candle-Out, and the mysterious Breeze for an Empty Room.

Some jars were filled with smoky black, gray, or silver swirls, others had brown bits and chunks of filth suspended in midair and several had faint sounds coming through the glass—like voices crying out in pain or laughter. A few were rocking, teetering, or rattling; these were secured to the wall by leather straps. But most of the thousands of jars were clear and still.

Aeolus glanced up at his almost endless collection. What concoction could he mix to please the great Hera? What was the right formula? High overhead was a jar labeled Hurricane Extract. But he'd already combined that with Tincture of Typhoon for this last storm and, to put it mildly, it didn't have the desired effect.

"How was I to know the girl had a magic rope?" he whispered to himself.

There were the winds he'd always counted on to

serve as the best foundations for his blends: Sirocco—Arabian Desert. Monsoon Additive. Tempest—Large. Tempest—Small. Zephyr Zest. Strong Wind Base. Gale Gel. Winds of Insanity. Mountain Pass Winds. Hot Air. Windbag. Wind for Shivers. Sudden Breeze.

He desperately wanted to use Thunderstorm Elixir, but knew that would require some of Zeus's lightning bolts and Hera had made it quite clear that not only was Zeus not to be involved in any way, but she didn't even want her husband to know.

"Do you want to know what I'll do to you if you tell him I was here?" she cooed to him when she'd requested the first storm.

"Oh gosh, lovely one, I really don't," Aeolus replied.

"Good, I'll tell you," Hera said. And she proceeded to explain just how hard it would be to mix winds with all ten of his fingers protruding from his backside and his nose stuck on top of his right knee.

Finally, Aeolus spotted a jar on one of the highest shelves; a jar with a tiny black funnel inside. He sighed deeply. Hera looked up at him and, following his gaze, rose immediately on her huge haunches.

"What? What is it? You've got your beady eyes on something!"

"Well," he said, ". . . it is something . . . it's just that it's not entirely ready! There's still more testing to be done!"

"What is it? We can test it on the girl. Go get it, get it!"

"Yes, gracious Hera. Notus! I need you—attend!"

A rush of the South Wind instantly filled the workroom and Aeolus was lifted off the floor, his dark robes flying and his long gray hair whipping in all different directions. He pointed to the glass jar with the tiny swirling funnel and was carried toward it like a weightless feather. He grabbed the jar and gave a quick little nod. He descended slowly and gently until at last his feet touched the floor.

"Thank you, Notus," Aeolus said as he crossed to the worktable, and the wind rushed outside once more. There was a soft tinkling of silver wind chimes in reply.

"Sheesh!" sneered Hera. "Such a production. I could have just snapped my fingers, you know. Had it on the table in an instant."

"The Queen of Heaven is too kind," Aeolus said, bowing low and trying not to sound irritated, "but we have our own little system. Perhaps a bit showy, yes, but it keeps Notus busy. We like to keep things moving around here, if you know what I mean."

"As you please," Hera said. Then she glanced at the jar Aeolus was holding and a wicked smile began to form. "Now what *is* that? Let me see it."

Slowly, Aeolus withdrew his arms from around the jar.

Inside was a small, black, circular funnel. The large end was at the top and a small point was moving back and forth across the bottom of the glass. It writhed and wriggled, twisting back in on itself like a serpent.

"Now *that* I like!" Hera clapped her hands together like a child. "I don't even know what it is, but I get a good feeling of destruction from it!"

"I call it a Tornado," Aeolus said. "I've only tested it once or twice, and not in the known world. I usually experiment on a terrain far across the ocean, where there are great plains and large expanses of flatland. The small end of the funnel touches the earth and plows a trough through anything it finds. And it sucks things, animals and trees and the like, up into the funnel, whirls them around for a bit, and then spits them out miles away."

"Now that's just genius!" Hera squealed.

"It still has a few glitches, though."

"Like what?" said Hera, although Aeolus could tell that her mind was already made up.

"Sometimes it inverts itself and the large end touches the earth. It's a little sloppier, not quite as delicate. Also, sometimes it just fizzles out. And then sometimes it doesn't touch the earth at all."

"I don't care, I love it! Use it!" said Hera.

"But . . . ," said Aeolus.

"I can still see to it that you give a whole new meaning to the phrase 'sitting on your hands'," she threatened.

"As Hera commands," Aeolus said quickly.

"Good! Use it immediately. Oh, I am so excited about this," Hera said, gathering her robes and preparing to leave. "Now I will show you how the great Olympians get around. None of this blowing to and fro on the top of a wind nonsense. Good day, Aeolus."

And with a giant puff of silver and blue smoke, the majestic Hera was gone, leaving only the sound of her voice purring hideously . . .

"And *this* time, it had better work!"

CHAPTER FIVE

A Shout

11:33 a.m.

Just at that moment, a cry went up from the top of the deck.

"Lighthouse! Lighthouse!"

The cry woke all three girls. Pandy from her musings on what lay ahead, and Alcie and Iole from their naps.

Alcie flew into the passageway, almost colliding with the captain on his way up to the top.

"All of you, on deck. Where's Homer? Hurry. One's first entrance into the Great Harbor at Alexandria is something not to be missed!"

The girls, with Homer following, jostled each other playfully as to who would be the first to reach the deck and set eyes on the magnificent lighthouse.

Dido won.

CHAPTER SIX

Tornado

11:34 a.m.

"I don't see it," said Alcie.

"Neither do I," said Iole.

"Hang on," said Pandy. "My dad told me about this . . . he's seen it lots of times. It starts off as a speck. Sometimes sailors are specially trained just to spot the lighthouse."

Pandy, Alcie, Iole, Homer, and Dido stood at the railing, all eyes searching the horizon for something different, strange, miraculous. All over the ship, sailors were making ready to put into port.

"Aren't they excited?" asked Alcie. "We're the only ones who seem to be excited."

"It's probably just another day to them," said Homer.

It was true; most of the sailors had made this voyage back and forth from Greece to Egypt many times before, so watching for the beacon of light that would guide the *Peacock* past the jagged rocks and into Alexandria was nothing to them. The girls, however, were ready to be in complete and total awe.

"Is that it?" said Iole. "No, it was just the sun reflecting off of a wave."

"What's that?" said Alcie, hopefully. "Oh, figs. Never mind. It's a fishing boat in the distance."

Suddenly, Dido gave a tremendous bark. And then another. And another.

Pandy knelt down by her dog. His eyes were almost completely white, so trying to follow his gaze was next to impossible; only a thin blue ring around his white irises told Pandy where to look.

"Where is it, ghost dog? Huh? Show me where," Pandy whispered into Dido's ear.

At that moment, a light sparked on the horizon. It disappeared and reappeared again and again as the ship rode through the small waves. But it was constant; always there when the ship crested high in the water.

The *Peacock* was still a good forty kilometers offshore, yet off in the far distance Pandy could see the brilliant light. It was a steady beam, like a true marker pointing the way into the Great Harbor.

"How does it do that?" Pandy asked of no one in particular. "What makes that light so bright in the daytime?"

"It's a mirror," said Homer. "They use a mirror to reflect the sun; that's why it's so bright."

"Apricots," said Alcie.

"And," continued Homer, "they light a fire at night and reflect that out to sea. The lighthouse is, like, one of the greatest architectural wonders in the world . . . right up there with the Hanging Gardens in Babylon. It's hundreds of years old."

"The coastline is so flat that ships would run aground if there was no guide into the harbor," Iole broke in, not wanting to be outdone in the brains department. "And there's a statue of Poseidon on the top . . . just in case anyone was curious."

"I was. Thanks," said Pandy.

The beam was getting stronger as the *Peacock* neared the harbor entrance. No one wanted to turn away from the beautiful buildings of Alexandria, now coming into view, but the light reflecting off the mirror was blinding.

"I'm going below deck to gather my stuff. I don't want to miss anything as we enter the harbor," said Iole.

"Right behind you," said Alcie. She turned to Pandy. "You coming?"

"I have my pouch," she replied, having gotten her leather carrying pouch and the box earlier. "I just have to get my water-skin."

"I'll bring it up," said Alcie.

"Okay, thanks. Ouch!" said Pandy, as a strand of her brown hair suddenly whipped into her eyes. "Where'd the wind come from?"

"Yeow!" said Alcie, her outer robe flying over her head.

"You look good that way," Iole joked to Alcie as she descended below deck.

"Oh, you are too funny!" said Alcie, fighting her fluttering robe and trying to follow. "Where are you?"

Then Iole, Alcie, and Homer were gone.

In the next instant, Pandy became aware that the sailors on the deck had shifted into high gear, many of them running about, grabbing ropes and tie lines. She looked up into the sky and saw not even a hint of a cloud. Then she heard one of the sailors speaking in Egyptian behind her. The urgency of his tone made her turn around and look.

Immediately, her eyesight shot past the sailor, out to the sea and sky behind the ship.

On the horizon about thirty kilometers away, back across the Ionian Sea that they'd just crossed, something hung in the air, the likes of which Pandy had never seen in her life.

It was a black funnel.

As she and the sailors watched in horror, the bottom of the funnel contorted and writhed back and forth, as if it were a soggy piece of cotton that someone high above was shaking hard. The funnel was, by Pandy's guess, at least a hundred meters wide at the top and two hundred meters high. Every so often the small point would touch down on the sea, sending water flying in all directions. Even at such a great distance everyone could see the massive amounts of water the funnel sucked up into itself, only to spit out again at deadly speeds. It was sucking other things up as well, and suddenly the *Peacock* was pelted by bits of low-flying seaweed and small rocks. A bird smashed into the main mast. Another hurtled like an arrow right at a sailor's head, knocking both man and bird senseless. Then a fish landed at Pandy's feet.

Worse still, the funnel was heading directly for the ship and gaining fast.

There was a tremendous wind created by the vicious whirling black monster. Even the most seasoned sailors were terrified; they were screaming and crying and praying fervently to Poseidon. Confusion and panic reigned on deck; no one knew what the hideous thing was. Rowing was out of the question; nobody would venture below deck for fear of being trapped. The only thought in anyone's mind was whether or not the *Peacock* could make it into the Great Harbor in time. But there was still too much distance between the ship and the barrier just beyond the lighthouse.

And the funnel, blocking out the sun, roaring and spewing and writhing, was now less than five kilometers away.

Alcie, Iole, and Homer came back on deck with all of

their belongings just as the ship, as if it weighed no more than a feather, spun in a full circle on the water.

"Hang on to something!" yelled Pandy.

Iole glanced for only half a second at the approaching funnel, then headed straight for the main mast, throwing her arms around the pole as tightly as she could. Homer knelt down at the railing and thrust his huge legs and arms through the poles, hugging them tightly.

Alcie had no choice but to hang on to Homer. She wrapped her arms and legs around his back, his robes blowing back over her face, blinding her.

Pandy lurched toward the mast pole, trying to throw her body around Iole, the wind whipping her hair violently into her eyes. Dido skidded in front of her path and ended by slamming hard into the shipping crates at the end of the deck. As Pandy turned her gaze to follow her dog, she looked up.

The funnel was upon them.

With a roar that made the sound of the first storm seem like a whisper, the funnel began to tear the sails, crack the mast, and blow the shipping crates to bits. Rigging ropes were airborne snakes and anything made of metal had the deadly force of a spear. Sailors began to fly into the air, sucked up forty and fifty meters high, then belched out again into the water far away, or hurled into the side of the *Peacock*, or back on deck, unconscious or dead.

Pandy, holding on to nothing, yet somehow standing stock-still in the middle of the funnel, felt the *Peacock* spin like a top as it was lifted out of the water and up into the gaping black mouth. She was struck dumb to her core, watching everything whirling around and feeling no wind, not realizing she was at the center of the tornado.

But just as quickly the small center point of the twister shifted and Pandy, with nothing to ground her, was thrown high into the air, becoming part of the furious, swirling storm. Her last clear vision was of the captain hanging on with one hand to the passageway entrance, his body completely horizontal to the ship's deck.

Pandy's mind went blank, except for one little thought: "This is how it must feel to be caught in a whirlpool." Except that whirlpools dragged you down into a wet spiral and she was being tossed higher on cold air currents in an ever-widening circle. Her arms and legs were whipping and smashing into the sides of her body. She caromed off something hard: another person, the top of the mast pole, a really big bird—she didn't know. She knew nothing except that now she had a shooting pain in her right arm, just below her elbow, and that these were probably her last moments alive.

All at once, she was flying through the air, arcing out

a hundred meters above the sea. Flashes of sunlight and deep blue water and light blue sky were all that met her eyes when she dared to open them. Then . . .

Smack!

She hit the water . . . and blacked out.

CHAPTER SEVEN

Rescue

12:09 p.m.

Pandy awoke underwater.

Light was filtering down through the waves from overhead, but it was getting dimmer, which could only mean that she was sinking. And there was absolutely nothing she could do about it. There was no moving her arms or legs, no swimming back to the surface; she was just too, too tired. Plus, there was a strange ache in one of her arms. She turned her head in the fading light and saw that her right arm was swaying in the current at an odd angle.

"Oh well," she thought. "This isn't exactly how I imagined it would all end, but there are worse ways to go."

Then she hit the bottom of the ocean.

She looked up and could still see the blue of the sky. But when she realized she was completely out of air, Pandy started to panic.

She didn't want to go! Not this way, not at all! Her life, suddenly and without warning, became very, very precious to her.

She struggled to move her left arm but it was caught in her robes and pouches. She tried kicking her legs, but the pressure of the water and her exhaustion made it too difficult.

She felt the last of the air leave her lungs.

The pain was incredible. Her throat seemed on fire. Just as she realized that not only would she never see her family or friends again, not only had she failed miserably in her quest, not only had she sentenced her family to eternal punishment, and on top of everything she didn't have any gold coins left to pay Charon to ferry her across the river Styx and into the underworld . . .

. . . the sunlight overhead got brighter.

And brighter.

And brighter.

She felt the pressure of the water around her lessen as something carried her toward the surface. Her head was thrown back and it bumped up against something sticking straight up behind her. Something flat and thick and curved.

A fin.

"Great," she thought, breaking the surface, her lungs now flat as two dried prunes. She hadn't landed on the sea floor after all; whatever it was was very much alive, and now she was going to be eaten.

She spit up whole mouthfuls of salt water, then gasped for air in tremendous, heaving gulps. Worn out from almost drowning and now about to be devoured, she rolled feebly to one side, trying to escape being a mid-meal.

But the thing with the fin rolled right along with her, keeping her afloat.

Pandy looked down. Gray, rubbery skin. Two flippers, one on either side. A huge dorsal fin (with her leather carrying pouch wrapped around it), coal black eyes, and a long pointed nose.

She was sitting on top of a dolphin.

"Hello-sorry-about-the-late-arrival-hope-you're-not-too-waterlogged-I-didn't-let-you-sink-too-far-so-you-shouldn't-be-feeling-any-ill-effects-I-see-you're-still-wearing-your-water-skin-but-your-leather-pouch-with-the-important-things-in-it-wink-wink-well-that-was-on-its-way-to-the-bottom-of-the-ocean-so-I-had-to-stop-and-pick-it-up-and-as-you-can-see-it's-quite-safe-around-my-fin-and-that's-actually-what-made-me-a-little-late-but-now-all-is-well-how-are-you?" it said, bobbing up and down in the water. The words came out so fast it was the same as hearing quick notes blown on a panpipe.

Pandy looked around her to make sure she hadn't

actually crossed into the underworld without knowing it. Was riding on the back of a dolphin—already enough of a shock—going to be her fate for eternity?

She saw the black funnel miles to the west, now small and distorted, as if it was running out of power. The lighthouse at Alexandria was a speck, barley recognizable by its teeny beacon of light. The *Peacock* was gone, and Pandy now saw splinters and shards of wood floating all about her.

"Hi-down-here-the-thing-you're-sitting-on-the-thing-that's-*talking*-to-you-I-said-how-are-you?" the dolphin repeated.

"Uh . . ."

"Oh, Great Artemis's Big Toe! Right . . . sorry, my fault! I forgot. Human, tiiiiny brain," said the dolphin, slowing his speech way, way down. "I basically just said, 'Hello, human.' You know, Poseidon warned us that you all might be a little untalkative, and a few of my fellow cetaceans think humans are just plain rude. But I think you're all quite nice for a species that uses just ten percent of the little brains Zeus gave you. And I don't mind saying so."

"I'm sorry," Pandy replied at last. "And I'm trying to use more than ten percent. I'm just not quite, um, sure where I am. I'm a little . . . like . . . oh, what's the word . . . ?"

"Disoriented?"

"Yeah! That's it."

"Not to worry!" said the dolphin, tossing his head merrily. "Do you have a name, human?"

"Yes."

"And . . . you'd like me to guess what it is?"

"Oh!" said Pandy. "No. Sorry. It's . . . um . . . Pandora."

"Well, Um-Pandora, I am Sigma, pleased to carry you. Ready?"

"No! Wait! For what? Ready for what?"

"We have to get you out of here," said Sigma. "We can chat a little later on. After all, we're going to be with each other for a while. Are your lungs up to taking a deep breath?"

"I think so."

"Good. You've ridden before, yes?"

"A dolphin?" said Pandy. "No, never."

"Ah, so you need the signs. Here you go."

Two dim violet-colored squares lit up on either side of the dolphin just behind his eyes. Within each square was written the words PLACE HAND HERE. Pandy put her hands directly on the squares; the skin here was loose and easy to hold. Instinctively, she grabbed large handfuls.

But as she tried to close her fingers, a sharp jolt shot through her right arm.

"Ow!" she cried.

"Pain?"

"Yeah . . . my arm."

"No wonder. You flew about sixty kilometers; water does *not* a soft landing make! Place your arm against my skin, Um-Pandora. Anywhere. Go ahead."

Pandy laid her arm against the dolphin's flank. She felt a small pulling sensation—as if her arm were being adhered to his skin—and a warmth moving from her elbow to her wrist. Sigma was silent for a moment. Then he shuddered slightly.

"You're in luck. It's just a sprain. Could have been worse!" he said. "I'll have it healed by the time we get there."

"There?"

"Later. Now, remember," said the dolphin, "*big* breath!"

Pandy inhaled as deeply as she could. The air rushing into her deflated lungs felt like she was sucking in nails; but something told her she'd better hold it in.

Sigma dove under the surface and shot forward with such speed that Pandy felt her lips part, the water flowing over her teeth and down her throat. She pressed her mouth closed. She hung her head to the side and flattened her body as best she could against the back of the big, beautiful mammal, surprised by how warm his skin felt against hers.

He didn't dive deep, only about two meters below the surface. After about ten seconds, he rose again.

"How was that?"

"I'm okay," Pandy answered. "I'm good . . . I think."

"Excellent! A little longer underwater this time. We'll take this slow. Breathe!"

She inhaled once more and he dove under the waves. This time he stayed under for almost twenty seconds.

"How're we feeling?" he said, resurfacing.

"I'm fine."

"You most certainly are, Um-Pandora! You're doing wonderfully well."

"My name isn't . . ."

"Now we'll try for twenty-five seconds," Sigma went on, "and if that's comfortable, we'll use that as a gauge all the way up."

"Up?"

"Later. Breathe!"

But twenty-five seconds was too much for Pandy's lungs.

"Ah," said Sigma. "We'll scale it back then. Get it? Scale? Fish? Ha! You see, I can say that because some of my best friends are fish!"

Friends!

"My friends!" said Pandy, realizing that she had forgotten about Alcie, Iole, and Homer.

And Dido.

"My dog!" she squealed.

"Nice pitch! You'd do well underwater," Sigma replied. "Look behind you."

Pandy twisted around.

In the distance, Homer was just breaking the surface on another dolphin, his hands firmly placed on the dim violet squares. The dolphin appeared to be having a little trouble keeping the huge youth stabilized; it already looked weary.

Before she could wonder why Homer had also been rescued, she caught sight of Iole, farther back, just emerging. Already, she and her dolphin rescuer were getting along famously. Iole's mighty brain was proving a delightful human exception, and the dolphin was chattering away furiously, lifting Iole in a graceful arc.

"Well, I have some pretty strong thoughts about the Pythagorean theorem myself, and I must disagree with you," Pandy heard Iole respond before she disappeared back into the sea.

Suddenly, on her other side, Pandy heard a shout. Whipping her head around, she saw Alcie, quite motionless, arguing with her dolphin.

"No . . . I got the hands part . . . with the little square thingies! But what about the feet? *Figs!* Where do I put my second left foot? Huh? This might come as a surprise, but I've got two left . . ."

Obviously out of patience, her dolphin snorted, Alcie screeched, and they both disappeared into the sea.

Then, to Pandy's right, Dido broke the water on the back of a small light gray dolphin. All four paws were planted firmly on four little violet squares. He turned for an instant to look at Pandy and gave two joyous barks before he went back under.

After coming so close to death yet again, Pandy had no idea why she would be smiling. But seeing her friends and her dog safe—ish—comforted her as if she were back at home on her own sleeping cot. She tossed her head back and let out a huge laugh.

"Satisfied?" said Sigma.

"Yes . . . thank you."

"And so we will be on our way. Breathe!"

Pandy took a deep breath and under they went. Rising and submerging, she grew comfortable enough after some minutes that she began to look around her, both above and below the water.

The group of dolphins was breaking the surface more or less together, although everything was dependent on each rider's lung capacity: Iole's small lungs required that she surface more often.

Above the waves, Pandy began to piece together a picture of where they were. If the lighthouse at Alexandria had been off to the west when she had first surfaced on Sigma and they were now swimming east, that meant . . . well . . .

She had no idea what that meant.

She became increasingly frustrated and very sorry that she had never really paid attention in Master Epeus's class when he was teaching geography; instead she had been staring out at the olive groves and doodling pictures of her heartthrob, Tiresias the Younger.

"Okay," she mused, "I must really think about it, reason it out . . ."

She remembered something vague about Egypt having a tremendous river flowing through it—the Nile. It branched off into two main tributaries as it neared the ocean (maybe she'd been paying a bit of attention after all). One went east, one went west. If Alexandria, closer to the west arm of the Nile, was behind them, and the sun was also behind them, then they were heading into the eastern arm of the river.

"Wow," Pandy thought, "I'm thinking like Iole."

But she had almost no time to be pleased with herself. The group of dolphins was slowing down, spending less and less time underwater with each dive. Finally they all came to a halt, forming a tight ring so everyone, dolphins and humans, could speak together without shouting.

"You guys all right?" asked Pandy quickly.

"I'm okay," said Iole, shivering slightly.

"Good," Homer replied.

Dido barked his agreement.

Everyone looked at Alcie.

"Apple skins and lemon rinds," she said finally, her curls soaked to her face like little snakes.

"Good!" said Pandy, smiling. "That was so completely aweso—"

"You'll forgive me," said Sigma, whose voice was now all business, "but we have no time for idle banter. We've stopped only to let each of you check to make sure you have everything of importance and then we're off. The Lord of the Sea said that we must hurry . . ."

"Poseidon?" said Pandy. "That's the second time you mentioned him. Did he send you?"

Black eyes flashed as the dolphins looked at one another.

"Of course," said another dolphin. "The Sea-God controls everything under the waves. Nothing is done without his knowledge."

"Then he's helping!" Pandy said excitedly. "You see, guys, we're getting help when we're not even asking."

"He revealed little to us of you specifically, Um-Pandora, or why you are so special to him," said Sigma. "Only that you all were tagged for retrieval and delivery."

"Excuse me," Homer said, looking at the dolphins and the girls, "but, like, why am I here? Not that . . . y'know . . . I'm not, like, grateful."

"Prudent question," Iole said looking at Pandy. "I was just *cogitating* the same thing."

"Maybe it's because he overheard us talking and the gods don't want anyone going around blabbing and frightening everyone about how the world's in such big trouble," Pandy replied.

"I wouldn't blab—"

"This is our quest, Homer. You don't have to come with us if you . . . ," Pandy began.

"He has to be here," said Alcie.

"He does?"

"I do?"

"The gods don't do anything without a reason, right?" Alcie went on. "Homer knows things we don't. He can do things we can't. He's been to gladiator school. He's bigger, stronger, and handso—bigger than us. We need him—or at least, we probably will—and the gods know that! So he stays."

Everyone stared at Alcie.

"I'm just saying," she said.

Homer thought only a moment: working in his father's import/export business or saving the world.

"I'm in."

"Look," said Pandy, turning to Sigma, "I mean . . . please, can't you tell us anything? At least tell us where we're going? You can do that, right?"

"I can tell you this much, Um-Pandora," said Sigma, who was clearly in charge. "We're members of DIA-SOZO. That means—"

"Rescue," said Iole.

"Right," said Sigma. "We're Poseidon's safety net for humans. We save those the great Water-God wishes. I'm Sigma. This is Delta, Iota, Omega One, and Zeta."

Each of the dolphins flipped their heads in turn.

"Alpha is scouting ahead and Omega Two has the rear . . . just to make sure we're not being followed."

"Who would want to follow us?" asked Homer.

"Hey! The first letters of each of your names spell out—," Alcie suddenly realized.

"Who would want to blow you out of the water? That's a better question," said Omega One, ignoring Alcie as he bobbed gently in the water with Iole on his back.

Pandy, Alcie, and Iole looked at each other silently; they each knew the answer.

"At any rate, all we know is that this is a diversion tactic. Other dolphins are rescuing the members of the crew so as not to give the appearance of favoritism, and they're whipping the water to create confusion. But we are the elite corps and, therefore, assigned to you," continued Sigma. "Our mission is to get you all up river and in country as soon as possible."

"You mean," Pandy said with a start, "we're going up . . . the Nile?"

"That's right," said Iota, wincing under Dido's sharp nails. "If I can handle the pain."

"You can handle it, soldier," said Sigma.

"Cool," said Homer. "How far?"

"That's on a need-to-know basis, human," said Zeta, who, with Homer on top, was almost completely submerged, but he gurgled his words as best he could.

"So," said Sigma. "All set?"

Pandy, Alcie, Iole, and Homer each checked their pouches. Suddenly Iole yelped.

"My father's sword! It's gone!"

"Do you need it?" asked Delta.

"I do," she said defiantly.

"Delta, contact Omega Two and tell him to search the sea floor for a human weapon of destruction. He'll know it when he sees it," said Sigma.

"Right," said Delta, as Alcie squirmed uncomfortably on his back.

"Let's go," Sigma called. The dolphins turned toward a vast expanse of water flanked in the distance by outcroppings of land on either side. Pandy could make out lush greenery; somehow they all had been carried closer to the shore than she'd thought.

"Group formation!" ordered Sigma, then each dolphin raised his head as they prepared to dive and said in unison . . .

"Breathe!"

CHAPTER EIGHT

Meanwhile...

1:05 p.m.

Prometheus stood very still on the stairwell. The only other people in the house—Sabina, the house slave, and Prometheus's young son, Xander—were napping in Xander's room.

So who was humming by the food cupboards?

He descended the stairs slowly. Being a Titan, he wasn't really afraid of anything it might be: a lost animal, a hungry wood nymph, a mischievous satyr. He was more curious than cautious.

Peering around the curve of the stairwell, he first saw a flash of silver toga. Then a jar of olives flew across the room as a huge forearm inadvertently swung out in the wrong direction.

"Oops."

Landing on the bottom stair, Prometheus watched the huge form dancing around the drainage counter, emptying something from a goatskin into two wooden bowls. He recognized the figure at once.

"So . . . I'll just pick up the olives, then, okay?" said Prometheus, wryly.

"Hey, pal!" Hermes whirled on his well-muscled leg. "Time for a snack."

"I'm not hungry."

"Yeah, yeah . . . worry, worry. Okay, here's the deal. Zeus has me delivering a message to a small temple in Athens and I asked if I could just, you know, check on you. Since I was gonna be down here anyway, right? He gives me the standard glare, but finally says yes. So on my way down I snuck by the food halls and snatched a little bit of Olympus for the two of us. Here."

Hermes, his winged helmet bumping against the ceiling, crossed the room with the bowls in his hand.

"Wow! Is this . . . ?" Prometheus asked, peering at the strange, shimmering concoction, inhaling the delicious aroma.

"You've been on earth so long you forgot already? That's ambrosia, pal! You eat. I'm gonna talk." Hermes was silent for a moment. He picked up a morsel of ambrosia and popped it into his mouth. "Your daughter? She's on the back of a dolphin."

Prometheus promptly choked on his food. Hermes whacked him on the back, sending him flying across the room into one of the wall frescoes.

"Oops."

"Say again?" Prometheus managed, picking himself up off the floor.

"Listen . . . you know Hera sent a storm to dump Pandora into the ocean about three days ago, but it didn't work, right?"

"Right. She told me about that two nights ago when she called."

"Well, this morning, just as the ship was approaching Alexandria, Hera made Aeolus send a bigger one. A real killer. And it nearly worked. Pandora hit the water with such a loud *smack,* we practically heard it up on Olympus."

Prometheus slumped. The thought of his baby girl in pain almost made him weep.

"No, it's good." Hermes saw the anguish on his friend's face. "Uncle P sent a few dolphins to pick up the kids and now everybody's ridin' high . . . and low . . . and high . . . so to speak. They're heading up the Nile. Not too far off the Alexandria mark. Well, about a hundred and fifty kilometers, but that's not a bad walk, right?"

"It's not a bad walk for you, fleet-foot. Or even me," Prometheus said. "But these are little girls. And that's a big, bad desert from what I remember."

"Which brings me to my point . . . you gotta tell her to be careful in the desert. Especially at first."

"Why? What's so dangerous that you had to sneak down to tell me?"

"Aphrodite passed Hera's rooms about an hour ago, right? And the Queen of Heaven is napping, but the goddess gums are flappin'. So Aphro changes herself into a fog and floats over Hera's bed to hear what she's saying. Between snores, Aphro manages to make out that Hera knows that your girl made it out of the sea and into the river, but she *doesn't* know all the details 'cuz Poseidon is keeping the whole thing on the hush-hush and Hera can't do anything to him anyway. So Hera knows the dolphins are gonna drop Pandora at some point, just not *exactly* where. So Hera's set more traps up and down the Nile. And from what Aphro says, they're doozies."

"Gods!"

"Aphro wasn't able to get any details. All she could make out were things like 'desert floor,' 'piles of bones,' and 'chamber of death.' That sort of thing. Oh, and something about big spikes."

"Spikes?"

"Yeah—those Egyptians, man!"

"What do I do?" Prometheus cried.

"Uh, gee . . . lemme think . . . um, shells?"

"Of course! I'll call her."

"You have to warn her."

"But it's daylight! If Zeus sees—"

"Pal, you either risk it or worry that Pandora will end up on the end of a large pointy piece of wood . . . or whatever they use down there."

"Where's my shell?" Prometheus raced upstairs to his sleeping chamber. "Where's my shell?"

"Good choice."

Hermes looked down at the uneaten ambrosia in Prometheus's bowl.

"Hey—you left some food in your bowl." Hermes quieted his voice to a whisper. "Do you still want it? Okay, I guess not. Do you mind if I eat it? Okay, I'm just gonna eat it then. Okay, thanks."

CHAPTER NINE
Up River
2:12 p.m.

One hour and innumerable dives later, between the salt water of the sea behind them and the current of the Nile pushing strongly against the dolphins, Pandy was a little surprised to find herself getting sleepy. She knew she dared not actually close her eyes; she was certain she'd lose the rhythm and inhale at the wrong time, gulping a lungful of river instead of the cooling afternoon air. Her arm, nestled against Sigma's flank, was now feeling almost completely normal, as if the dolphin had taken all the pain of her sprain into his own body, leaving her healed. She decided to risk lifting it just for a moment in order to turn and check on the others. Iole, off to the left, was now chatting slowly and quietly with Omega One. Pandy heard her mention the name of the great teacher, Plato, then Iole gave a loud quick laugh and Omega One tossed his head in the air, giggling as he crashed down into the water.

"She's so smart," Pandy mused as Sigma again took her below, and then she smiled to herself; if she couldn't have the biggest brain in the world, at least it belonged to one of her best friends.

Surfacing again, she turned to her right. Alcie was staring straight ahead, a mellow expression on her face. Her mouth was moving ever so slightly and Pandy thought for a second that Alcie might be figuring out the best way to curse her when this whole adventure was over . . . if they ever got back home. Then Pandy heard a faint tune and realized that Alcie was singing. It was nothing recognizable; probably something she'd learned aboard ship. Alcie glanced at Pandy and waved. Pandy immediately raised her right arm and wiggled her fingers in response without any ache at all. She gazed at Alcie's two left feet twisted on the dolphin at miserable angles. The idea of the pain that Alcie was willingly putting herself through for the sake of their friendship hit her like a stone in the chest. She didn't allow herself tears; instead; she felt quite honored.

She craned around to look at Homer, riding surprisingly high on his dolphin. Then she realized that it wasn't Zeta, his original dolphin, at all. Zeta was swimming close by in formation and as Pandy watched, Homer's new dolphin took him under the waves but it was Zeta who came up with him again. Then, after Zeta carried the heavy youth for a few minutes, Homer was passed back to the second dolphin.

Far to her left, Dido was curled up on Iota's back, eyes open and alert. Dido saw his young mistress look at him and gave short bark, letting Pandy know he was fine before settling his head again on Iota's flank.

But over the next two hours, even the soft singing and quiet conversation stopped as the dolphins focused all their strength on maintaining top speed. Everyone began to feel the strain of the journey. The banks of the Nile were still lush and green the farther up river they got; Pandy remembered learning that in some places along its banks the soil was so fertile that Egyptian farmers could grow two crops on the same land in one year, almost unheard of in Greece. But beyond the green reeds and trees there were flat expanses of light brown, broken by the occasional light brown hill or light brown mountain. They passed small villages with light brown homes. Every so often they passed enormous light brown buildings with massive columns, not unlike their own temples back in Greece.

Just as Pandy let her mind drift toward thoughts of home, she felt a small vibration in the middle of her back. Then it was gone. And then it began again.

"Excuse me, Um-Pandora," said Sigma, "but you're jiggling. Perhaps you picked up a fish when you landed in the water? An eel, maybe? Or a shrimp?"

"I don't think I . . . oh, I know!"

She twisted to reach her leather carrying pouch, attached securely to Sigma's dorsal fin. Slowly and carefully, she removed the vibrating conch shell and quickly closed the pouch again. During her next arc above water, she ran her finger down the shell lip and held it to her mouth.

"Hi-Dad-hang-on," she managed to sputter just before going under again. She could hear her father's voice coming through the shell even several meters underwater.

"Daddy-I-can't-talk-now."

She heard a muffled "Where are you now?" on the other end of the conch.

"I'm-on-a-dolphin-in-the-river."

"Pandora, listen . . ." She heard him more distinctly this time.

"I'm-okay-I'll-talk-to-you-later."

"Pandora, I have to tell you someth—"

"Bye-Dad-big-time-phileo."

She put the conch back into her pouch.

Some minutes later, she began to wonder what was so important that her father would risk using the shells in the middle of the day, and risk the great Zeus finding out that Prometheus could communicate with his daughter. She glanced about, looking for anything out of the ordinary.

Out of the ordinary.

"Now *that's* funny!" she thought.

Soon after they skirted by a rather heavily populated village, rousing alarmed shouts from children playing along the riverbank, they came to a long stretch of land on the right that appeared completely deserted. It looked as if it had been a well-used port at one time, and there was an enormous pile of fallen sandstone that had obviously once been a temple.

Sigma slowed again and glided smoothly toward the bank.

All of a sudden, Pandy's feet touched the river bottom, creating murky swirls in the shallow water as her sandals dragged through the mud. Alcie, Iole, and Homer pulled alongside but Dido, eager to be on dry land, leaped off of Iota and quickly dog-paddled to shore.

"Here you are, Um-Pandora," Sigma said, the cheery tone returning to his voice. "This is where we have been instructed to deposit you. Your arm is well, yes?"

"Yes, thank you," she replied, rubbing it instinctively. Not even a twinge.

"Very good," Sigma said. He turned toward Iole as another dolphin swam up to the group, a short silver object slung around its dorsal fin.

"I believe this is what you asked for, is it not?"

"My father's sword!" she cried, taking the blade. "Thank you . . . um . . . ?"

"Omega Two," the dolphin answered.

"Thank you very much, Omega Two."

"Zeta, Alpha," Sigma addressed the pair of dolphins who'd borne the weight of Homer for over a hundred kilometers. "Nicely done."

"Pfft . . . mfft . . . uhh," was all Alpha could muster. Zeta was too tired to reply and just floated on his back.

"All right, humans—everyone off!" Sigma said. Each dolphin rolled to the right, gently dropping its rider into the Nile.

"Grapes." Alcie popped her head out of the water. "They might have warned us that was coming."

As the group stood up, getting their bearings and collecting their belongings, the dolphins began to move toward the deeper center of the river.

"Thank you!" called Pandy.

"Be well, Um-Pandora. Stay safe!" came Sigma's reply.

"Hey!" Pandy cried. "Where are we?"

"Egypt!" he called as he disappeared.

There was silence for about ten seconds as the group watched the dolphins swim back downriver. Then, as if on cue, Alcie opened her mouth.

"Duh!"

CHAPTER TEN

And Meanwhile...

3:17 p.m.

"She hung up on me."

"She's in the middle of the Nile," said Hermes, his mouth full of the last of the ambrosia.

"I can't believe that she couldn't listen for just a moment."

"Yes, Prometheus," Hermes continued, his finger wiping the inside of the wooden bowl. "She's an ungrateful child and must be flogged."

He paused, cleaning his teeth with his little finger.

"Oh, for Artemis' sake, my friend, she's having a rough go at the moment. I'm sure she'll use the shell the instant she gets onto dry land."

"I have to call her back . . ."

"Look, I'm all for your eldest not getting killed and I know this is important, but just give it a minute. Sustained activity in the same location might draw unwanted attention, hint-hint. She's still in the water, so she's okay for right now. And she's too curious not to wonder, so she'll call you back!"

"Of course she will," said Prometheus softly, staring out the window.

"That's it!" Hermes rose from the floor cushion on which he'd been sitting (popping the seams and squeezing out the feathers). "You're coming with me. Your daughter's been gone roughly three weeks and I happen to know you've been outside exactly twice in that time. Dirty toga, beard needs trimming. And you have obviously forgotten the verb 'bathe' . . . as in 'to bathe' . . . as in 'you need to bathe.' Your atrium business is going to Hades . . . not that it really matters, since Pandora loosed evil into the world I know orders have been down, but that's not my point. She's taken this on and so far, she's doing fine. And—must I remind you—you have a son who still needs a father. So, we'll deliver the message to the temple, delight in the awe I generate, get you to the baths so you stop smelling like the Athens waste pit, and get you into a fresh toga. Now shape up and grab hold of my arm. We're off!"

"But when she calls . . ."

"Bring the shell, for Olympus' sake!"

Prometheus knew better than to argue; he also knew his oldest friend was absolutely right. He'd been completely neglecting everything for weeks. Food was left uneaten, the news in the *Daily Scroll* went unread, and evening prayers to his favorite gods and goddesses went unuttered. Sabina, the house servant, who was usually deferential (if slightly cantankerous) had handed him a broom two days earlier, telling him to get up off his sleeping pallet and either sweep the entire upstairs or the downstairs, she didn't care which as long as he was moving. And, worst of all, his son Xander began to have a rather startled look when Prometheus approached, as if the tall bearded man were a complete stranger.

He gave Hermes a tired, acquiescent smile and put the shell into the folds of his dirty toga.

"Take me where you will."

"Oh, the sights you'll see . . . ," Hermes joked.

But as Prometheus grabbed Hermes' arm, the instant, violent rush of their departure shook loose the little conch from the folds of fabric. It arced unseen into the air, landing with a soft thud on one of the floor cushions.

Where it lay. Waiting to vibrate.

CHAPTER ELEVEN

Egypt

4:00 p.m. (exactly)

Pandora Atheneus Andromaeche Helena, who, only less than a few weeks before, had never ventured farther than the Athens city limits, stepped out of the Nile River and onto the sandy soil of Egypt. There was lush greenery far off to her right and left; plants and trees drinking in the Nile. But straight ahead of her lay a large deserted stretch of sand, leading to a huge abandoned temple about two hundred meters away. Beyond that there was nothing but the open desert.

"I can't believe I'm actually saying this, but it feels good to walk," Alcie said.

"Is everyone all right? Everybody have everything?" Pandy asked.

Homer wrung the river water from his garments.

"I'm good."

"I'm excellent," said Iole. "But a little tired. I have never talked so much in my life. Quite stimulating."

"Yeah, you and Omega One were blabbing the entire time. My dolphin made me be quiet," said Alcie.

"I have to talk to my dad," said Pandora, retrieving the conch shell. "He was trying to tell me something."

She traced her forefinger down the lip, which she knew would activate her father's shell.

"Dad?" she said quietly. Even hundreds of kilometers from Greece, she knew that Zeus and Hera might be gazing down upon her at any time. Alcie and Iole raised their voices to cover Pandy's whisperings. They knew there would be big trouble for everyone if the two most powerful gods caught Pandy getting help from her father.

"Say . . . um," Alcie yelled to Homer, "this is a very . . . uh . . . brown country, don't you think?"

"Uh-huh," said Homer. Then he just stared blankly at Alcie.

"Thank you, Homer! Iole, your thoughts?" Alcie called.

"I believe the word you're looking for is 'ecru,' Alcie," said Iole, loudly.

"Yes, of course, ecru . . . that's it!" Alcie replied.

In Pandy's home in Athens, her father's conch shell lay on the floor cushion where it had landed, vibrating furiously.

"Ah, yes. Ecru. Of course now that I really look at that temple, for instance, I think it's more of a dirt color," Alcie cried.

"It's umber, mixed with taupe!" said Iole.

"It's an umber-y, taupe-y dirt!" Alcie was getting so loud, Pandy was certain that if the gods weren't already looking in their direction, Alcie's voice would make sure they did.

"Guys . . . guys! You can stop yelling," Pandy said, replacing the conch shell in her pouch. "He's not answering."

"Well, couldn't have been anything too important then, right?" said Alcie.

"I don't know. But he wouldn't call in the middle of the day for no reason. My curiosity is tingling," Pandy said.

"He'll call again, I'm sure," said Iole.

"Right!" said Pandy, surveying her new surroundings. "Okay . . . I've been thinking. Three hours ago, we were almost to Alexandria and the sun was overhead."

She began to pace forward and backward. Walking toward the ruined temple and back again.

"Then the storm flung us that way and the DIASOZO picked us up and carried us *that* way. And the sun was there," indicating a point overhead.

"And we traveled this way and the sun is now there . . . which means that Alexandria is . . . is . . ."

She paused, walking just a little closer to the temple, then Pandy turned back toward her friends.

"Go on, Pandy, you're doing great!" said Iole.

"Thank you. Which means that Alexandria is . . . that way!"

She flung her left arm defiantly (and with great flourish) off to one side.

She seemed so confident in her decision that all eyes, even Dido's, turned obediently toward the direction in which she pointed, as if the rooftops of the great Egyptian city would somehow be visible.

"Way to go, Pandy!" said Alcie. "That's the way I would have . . ."

Alcie turned back.

"Pandy?"

"Pandy?" said Iole.

Dido gave a series of short, sharp yelps.

Pandy was gone.

"Pandy!" Iole screamed.

"Where did she go?" asked Homer.

"Oh, Gods! Pandy!" yelled Alcie.

Dido shot like an arrow toward the spot where, not one second before, Pandy had stood. But before he reached the precise spot, he skidded to a stop and began to whimper, as if there were a snake in the sand in front of him.

Iole ran to his side.

"Where is she, boy?" she asked, half hoping that Dido would be able to tell her. She looked hard at the place where Pandy had been. And then she saw something.

"Do you think she's playing a game? Pandy! It's not funny!" Alcie bumped softly into Iole as she came to stand alongside.

"Shh!" Iole said. "Don't move. Look."

"Where?"

"There."

Sure enough, there was a gently sloping indentation in the sand, like a shallow funnel. Grains of sand were still flowing down into the center as if something had reached up and sucked Pandy down into the desert floor.

"Oh, great Zeus, she's drowning!" shrieked Alcie. "Get her rope!"

"She's got the rope!" said Iole.

Alcie spun around.

"Homer! Homer—help!"

But Homer was crossing the barren sand with the speed of a chariot stallion. Alcie watched, mouth agape, as he raced up the broken steps of the temple three at a time.

"Where are you going?" she shouted.

"Come on!" he cried, his voice lost as he reached the top step.

Of all the new sensations Pandy had experienced in the last few weeks, this was definitely one of the worst. The desert floor had simply given way under her feet. But unlike the momentary sensation of falling through thin air that she had felt up on Olympus, she was immediately surrounded by heaps of sand closing in on her. She'd heard of quicksand, but in real quicksand, one was actually drowned, suffocated slowly. Now, as she fell fast through the earth, the sand clogged her nose and scraped her skin. Inadvertently, she opened her mouth to scream as the last of the daylight disappeared and sand poured into her mouth. And still she was falling.

Suddenly, instantly, the sand thinned around her and she was hurtling downward into blackness. In spite of her terror, she became aware of a putrid stench.

Then she heard a loud rip of fabric and felt something solid pushing against her left hip as she fell, grating her skin.

She crashed into something hard but brittle, slowing her fall as it shattered.

And then she hit the ground. She hoped. Whatever she had landed on was sharp and jagged, like a pile of rough pieces of wood or rock. She lay there, drifting in and out of consciousness, fighting to stay awake. The stench was helping; it reminded her of the oil her mother would inhale whenever she felt "faint." Pandy began to move slowly, lifting her head in the darkness and laying it down again. She moved her arms and legs, checking for any jolts of pain. There were none, which she knew meant that nothing was broken. She felt her hip; there was a stinging that made her gasp and it was wet. She brought her hand to her mouth and inhaled: blood. She spat out the last of the sand and tasted the wetness. She was bleeding, all right. Then her hand brushed again something hard, circular, and sticking straight up in the air. A pole? A thin column?

Just as she began to sit up, she was aware of a flash of light behind her, which lit the chamber in which she lay. She turned her body slowly.

An enormous object floated about twenty-five meters away. A glowing blue sphere surrounded a strange symbol of curved black lines in the shape of a terrible eye, almost like the eye of a bird, the whites on either sides of the black iris gleaming with pure energy.

Then she heard a voice.

"Ah . . . fresh blood!"

Dido was already on the move as Alcie and Iole ran to follow Homer. They crossed the fifty or so meters in seconds and hurried up the steps. On top of the large front terrace, past thick carved stone columns, four enormous seated, decaying statues gazed out over the cracked flagstones onto the desert. Each had a strange headdress and a square stone beard. There was an opening in the wall between the ankles of each statue. Homer was darting back and forth between the four entryways, talking to himself.

"Here—that goes into the temple. Or does this one go into . . . ? This might lead . . ."

"Homer?" said Alcie.

"Quiet please," he replied. Then he raced forward into one of the two middle entryways. "Here!"

Iole and Alcie and Dido followed silently. Shortly inside the passageway, Iole saw Homer waiting for them.

"Hold my cloak; we don't want to get separated."

Iole clenched a fistful of cloak in one hand and Alcie's wrist in the other.

Homer moved quickly in the growing dark, feeling his way along the wall, which sloped down at a sharp angle.

"Stay close to the left wall."

"Trying," said Alcie.

"How do you know where you're going?" asked Iole.

"Field trips."

"Huh?" said Alcie.

"When I was at gladiator school in Ethiopia, sometimes we'd get to go on field trips if we did really well in basic strategy or hacking class. I've been in temples like this before. They don't treat their dead like we do back in Greece. Especially those they want to keep an eye on."

"Keep an eye on?" said Alcie.

"You know, like thieves, murderers, grave robbers. After they've been punished, their bodies are thrown into a large room called the 'Chamber of Despair.' It's usually off to the side of the temple, underneath the desert. Pandy must have fallen through the ceiling. One of the four passageways up on the main portico would have led down to it. I just hope I picked the right one. We'll know soon."

"How?" asked Iole. "It's pitch black."

As if in answer to her question, the most horrible smell imaginable wafted into her nostrils. Alcie broke out of Iole's grip and covered her nose with both hands.

"What in Apollo's name is that?" she cried.

"It's exactly what I hoped for," said Homer. "When I said they just tossed the bodies in, that's like totally what they did; one on top of another. That's the smell of a burial chamber."

"Alcie, where are you?" Iole said sharply.

"I'm here," Alcie replied, fumbling in the dark for Iole's free hand. "I can't breathe, but I'm here."

"Cover your noses, breathe with your mouths," said Homer. "I just hope she landed on a body and not anything else."

"What do you mean?" asked Iole.

"Well, thieves and grave robbers and such were executed by . . . like . . . impaling. And often the stakes were still in the bodies when they tossed them in the chamber. Quiet—we're almost there."

But Alcie and Iole were already silent as statues as they prayed to every god and goddess they could think of that Pandy hadn't ended up skewered like a lamb roast.

Suddenly the passageway lit up with a soft glow only a short distance ahead.

Alcie glanced at the wall next to her: a human skull, set into the wall, stared back at her. She was about to scream when she heard a loud voice.

"Ah . . . fresh blood!"

CHAPTER TWELVE
The Chamber of Despair
4:28 p.m.

The entire chamber was now glowing murky white. Pandy stared at the unblinking eye, floating in midair. It was easily ten meters in diameter and the lines surrounding it gave it a fierce, enraged appearance. But after the first words echoed through the chamber, words Pandy did not understand in the least despite Egyptian 101 back at school, all was eerily quiet.

Slowly, she began to look around, careful not to move too much should the eye see her and speak again.

What she saw was terrifying. The chamber stretched into darkness on both sides, and there was a wall of dark bones about forty meters directly in front of her; finger, hip, and leg bones jutting out at every possible angle. But the floor of the chamber . . . that was something entirely different.

Whole bodies. Thousands of them. Scattered. Piled. Stacked one on top of another forming dozens of small hills that faded into the black of the chamber. Most were already skeletons or severely decayed and as she looked, several leg and foot bones simply dropped off, crashing to the floor below.

She closed her eyes tightly, wanting to block out the sight around her.

Had she really just seen what she thought she'd seen? As a little girl, her father had told her stories of fierce battles, great scenes of destruction and death (before her mother had whacked him on the head and told him to stop), so she could pretty well handle the thousands of human bones strewn about. But had she really seen the . . . holes? Every body that she'd glimpsed, she thought, had a hole in its mid-section.

She slowly opened her eyes and looked up. All over the chamber light radiated through the bones, causing spooky silhouettes. But in some places, small discs of filmy white, like little moons, could be seen as the light from the giant eye shone through the perfectly round circles in the bodies.

Except, of course, for the bodies with huge wooden poles through the middle.

Pandy gasped.

Directly in front of her were the bones of a man lying twisted and curved around a thick wooden pole.

There were hundreds of poles all over the chamber, their ends sharpened to fine points. Half had toppled over, but half were still upright. She had assumed that these were only support poles, shoring up the desert floor high above and keeping it from caving in. But each pole carried a human skeleton somewhere on its shaft. The pole she was lying against didn't have a body. Then she realized the crunchy bits underneath her were the remains of a skeleton she had crashed into as she fell.

Then, from off to her right, she heard the murmur of voices, very soft, but getting louder and talking fast. Turning her head she saw a small flash of white fur and three larger shapes burst into the chamber from a dark entryway.

"Pandy?"

"Kumquats! Pandy, where are you?"

She was opening her mouth to answer when a pulse in the light made her glance back toward the horrible eye.

The eye had turned slightly, rotating toward the new sound coming into the chamber. A beam of light shot out from the center of the eye toward the four figures and the same loud voice shouted again.

"Enter not, dogs! You will wait until you are needed!"

Suddenly, it seemed to Pandy that her friends had slammed up against an invisible wall. She could see Iole's arms outstretched, her hands pressed flat against an unseen barrier. Alcie, trying to find some way around, was only succeeding in smashing her nose on something she just couldn't see. Homer was throwing his entire weight against . . . whatever it was . . . again and again. Dido, Pandy saw, was rigid, barking furiously, his white eyes focused on her lying on the pile of bones.

The eye turned back toward Pandy, now almost on her feet.

"You disturb the chamber. You are of flesh. This is not allowed."

Silence.

Pandy looked again to her friends, scuttling noiselessly like beetles inside an invisible jar. Could she get to them? Could she free them . . . or herself?

"You disturb the chamber. You are of flesh. This is not allowed."

"I . . . I . . . don't understand what . . . ?"

Pandy stood, half hiding behind the pole, and accidentally grazed her left hip against the wood, causing a sharp spasm of pain. She twisted around the pole to peer out from its other side. As she did, she caught sight of a figure, ducking down behind a pile of corpses about thirty meters away.

"Hello?" she cried before she realized that calling attention to herself in front of someone who may or may not want to kill her just might be the most idiotic thing she could do.

The light around the eye pulsed again and again. Each burst getting brighter.

"Speak not, desecrator," the voice boomed. "Prepare to join those who have gone before!"

Suddenly, the sound of several voices filled the chamber, repeating a single phrase again and again.

"What is this thing?" cried Iole behind the invisible barrier.

"What is *that* thing?" said Alcie, pointing to the huge eye, now focused on Pandy.

"Homer? Homer! Stop it!" said Iole, stepping in front of Homer as he prepared to charge again. "You obviously can't break through. We're trapped. This thing, this invisible wall, is magic of some kind . . . or the work of the gods."

"Hera's found us," whispered Alcie.

"Hera wouldn't be able to act this fast, at least I don't think so," said Homer, panting hard as he slumped against the barrier.

"What do you mean?" asked Iole.

"This is Egypt. The people have their own gods. Like . . . different ones."

"I know *that* part," said Iole.

"But . . . like . . . if Hera wanted to get to you, she'd have to get permission from Isis, or Osiris, Nut, Ka, Geb. Maybe even Anubis. Our gods can't just come in and take over. They have to ask." Homer suddenly charged the invisible wall again. "Ugh . . . I think there might even be paperwork."

"It's glowing brighter again!" said Alcie, looking at the eye.

"Nephthys prepares a place. Kneel before Nephthys," the voice said, the sound ricocheting off the walls of the chamber.

"I can't . . . I can't understand! Something about kneeling in place," cried Iole, listening intently. "I dropped Egyptian 101 for Basic Chinese!"

"It's a chant. It's saying 'Nephthys prepares a place. Kneel before Nephthys,'" said Homer.

"Who's that? What's that mean?" asked Alcie.

"The Egyptian Goddess of the Dead. They pray to Nephthys before they sacrifice or execute someone."

"Great Apollo!" gasped Iole.

"But it makes no sense," said Homer, pacing and pointing to the huge eye. "That's the Eye of Horus. It's a symbol of healing and protection. The Egyptian students at school wore it around their necks. It doesn't destroy anything!"

Dido began whimpering, turning in small circles then putting his paws up against the invisible wall.

"Figs," said Alcie, turning, "look!"

Pandy's knees buckled under her, as if someone had hit the back of her legs with a rod, and she lost complete control of her body. Her head was thrown back, her arms were flung up then thrust violently forward as her body was bent so her face and arms hit the floor. Then, still on her knees, her upper body was raised up and thrown back, then slammed forward again into the ground.

"What's happening to her?" screamed Iole, prying a rock loose from the entryway to the chamber.

"I don't know!" cried Homer, pacing again rapidly back and forth. "Something's making her move like that. Usually people . . . prisoners and stuff . . . don't have to be told, they just kneel and pray before they're killed. But she doesn't know the custom, so something's making her do it anyway."

"They pray?" cried Alcie, now hitting the barrier with her pouch while Iole was smashing it with a rock and Dido was pawing at the ground, trying to tunnel underneath.

"They want to be safe in the realm of the dead! I don't know. It's just what I learned at . . ."

"Gladiator school!" they all cried together.

Suddenly Iole stood very still and looked straight up.

"Homer—put me on Alcie's shoulders!"

"Huh?"

"Put me on Alcie's shoulders!" said Iole again. "I want to see how high this wall goes. Maybe that *thing* out there didn't make the wall quite as high as it should have. If I can get over, I'm gonna try to get around behind the eye . . . and . . . disturb it . . . distract it somehow. Maybe it will be enough to rescue Pandy."

"Or send us into a fiery death," said Alcie.

"Yes, fine! Maybe! Whatever! Homer, now . . . please?" said Iole, looking at Homer, who was staring at Pandy flopping wildly.

"Oh . . . yeah, got it," he said, turning back.

Over and over, Pandy was being forced by some power to bow and scrape. With each thrust forward, her face was scratched by shards of bone and small rocks. She lost track of how many times she bowed; lost track of time, lost track of her friends. She tried to keep her eyes open, but the alternating between light and dark made her nauseated. She was on the verge of passing out when, suddenly, the flopping stopped. She was bent over forward and her legs shot out from underneath. Lying facedown in the dirt, her mouth filling with dust, her body was as inflexible as a piece of marble. The chanting, she realized, had never ceased. But now it had altered. It didn't matter, because she still had no idea what it meant.

And then she was off the floor.

She felt herself lifted into the air, her limbs now limp and dangling. She was being raised as if she were on an invisible platform. Pandy opened her eyes and saw the ground fading away. She didn't think to scream, but she was vaguely aware of her stomach making small gurgling noises. She drifted past the skeletons hanging on the poles, rising above them and seeing just how sharp and fine the pole points were. Now she saw the entire chamber. In the dim light, surrounded by long-unused oil lamps, were enormous colored murals on three of the walls. Strange figures with arms at sharp angles seemed to be walking in a line toward a large figure seated on a chair. Their hands held plates of food stacked like little pyramids. There were hundreds of bizarre bird profiles and dozens of eyes, including a symbol that resembled the terrible eye now far below her.

Suddenly she was being pushed backward. She looked underneath her as best she could.

"Oh no!" she cried.

CHAPTER THIRTEEN

Aloft

5:11 p.m.

"I can't even stand up straight as it is. How am I gonna carry—oof," said Alcie, as Homer, as if he were picking up a kitten, scooped Iole off the ground and sat her square on Alcie's shoulders.

"Now, Homer, put Alcie—"

"I know, I know. I'm not . . . like . . . totally without brains, okay?" said Homer, who lifted Alcie by her knees and placed her two left feet on his shoulders. He locked his hands around the backs of her knees to hold her in place.

"Now walk forward slowly," said Iole, her arms in front of her.

Homer inched his way toward the invisible wall, balancing the two girls as if they were a basket of feathers on top of his head.

"I'm not even gonna ask where you learned to do this," said Alcie, her arms tightly gripping Iole's legs.

"Take a guess," said Homer, stepping forward on his right foot. "Ow!" he cried, "I hit something . . . and I stubbed my toe."

"Oh, *puh-leeze*," said Alcie.

"Did you hit the wall?" asked Iole.

"I guess so."

"It's there! It's right in front of me," said Alcie, extending her hand.

"I don't feel anything," said Iole, excitedly, wiggling her fingers. "I've got nothing up here! It doesn't go all the way up!"

She felt around the space in front of her, finally locating the top of the invisible wall. From touching it at every possible angle, she determined that it was about one meter in width; enough room to sit on comfortably before she dropped to the other side.

"Okay, I'm going over!" Iole said, pulling herself onto the wall and accidentally kneeing Alcie in the neck.

"Ow! Apricots. Wait!"

"Yeah, wait," said Homer.

"Why?" Iole asked.

Homer and Alcie paused.

"I've got nothing," said Alcie.

"Me neither," replied Homer.

"I'm gone!" and Iole sat on the wall for only a moment before she lowered herself down, coming face-to-face with Alcie on the other side. Their eyes locked and Iole saw Alcie mouth the words, "good luck." But knowing Alcie, Iole thought, she probably yelled it at the top of her lungs.

"So," Iole mused, "the wall is a sound barrier from *this* side."

She dropped easily to the main floor of the chamber just as Alcie began to pummel Homer to put her down again.

As she turned and looked up, Iole's heart dropped into her stomach. While they had been focused on getting over the invisible wall, no one noticed Pandy being hoisted fifty meters into the air.

The razor-sharp point of the nearest pole was coming into view underneath her, perhaps only five meters below.

When the point was aimed directly up at Pandy's stomach, she stopped. And hovered.

For a second.

And then she felt herself descend. Very, very slowly.

She wanted to flail wildly but her body was still rigid and out of her control. She could only watch as the pole grew closer. She was going to be pushed onto the point and left there until she was nothing but a pile of bones crashing to the floor.

And there was absolutely nothing anybody could do about it.

Homer had tried to put Alcie down as swiftly and gently as he could. He used a right-handed, right-footed dismount assist, standard when undoing a human ladder, and it had always worked back in school. Unfortunately he hadn't ever used it on someone with two left feet. Alcie had toppled backward on Homer and was now hanging upside down with Homer's huge hands trying to get a firm grip on her two left ankles.

But even hanging upside down and furious as a sea nymph on dry land, she still managed to take in what was happening beyond the wall.

"Homer . . . looook!"

The fear Pandy felt was unbearable. However, as soon as she realized what was in store for her, she became aware of something behind the fear.

Anger.

Back home in Greece she had understood all that had happened to her and her friends. At the Temple of Apollo, when Callisto, the high priestess, had been about to roast Iole over the great altar fire, Pandy understood that Callisto thought they were thieves. And Callisto had been driven to insanity by the Jealousy she was carrying inside. Pandy had at least been able to talk to, if not reason with, the high priestess. Now, here in Egypt, she had no idea why any of this was happening. And her fear turned into rage and frustration.

At least when Callisto had ordered Iole's death, it was in plain Greek and Pandy could do something about it. She could put out the flames underneath Iole using her newly discovered power over fire.

She was now only two meters above the top of the wooden pole.

The wooden pole.

Wood.

Which burns.

Could she do it?

She could flash small, cold embers into tiny fires back in her own room, but could she . . . ?

The point was now only one meter away.

Pandy concentrated all her thought and energy, focusing everything she had on the pole.

"Send the force down," she thought. "Shatter and burn. Shatter and burn. Shatter and burn."

And, like that day in the temple, she again went deaf. The world around her was utterly silent and she no longer heard the chanting or the shattering of bones dropping off the mounds.

But this time she knew exactly what was happening and her heart gave a little leap in her chest.

Her nose caught a small whiff of smoke. Something burning! Something on fire! She had no time to rejoice, though, and started concentrating even harder.

The point of the pole, so close now, began to glow a dull red, then brightened into an incandescent orange. Pandy forced her chin into her neck as she struggled to keep the point in sight below her. Suddenly the point flared into flame and Pandy felt the heat on her belly through her silver girdle; not painful in the least, more like the gentle caress of fine silk blowing in a breeze.

The fiery pole was now piercing the folds of her toga and pressing against her belly button. And still she was being lowered.

She allowed herself a small, fierce smile and focused with every ounce of strength in her mind.

Then the razor point pricked her stomach. Pandy closed her eyes and gave a yelp. Then she felt a vibration in her belly as the pole began to shake violently. Her eyes flew open and she watched in astonishment as a streak of white-hot fire split the entire shaft neatly down the middle. Her hearing returned just in time to hear the pole crash into piles of bone at either end of the chamber, sending hunks of ancient wood flying in every direction.

"Great Aphrodite, blessed Apollo, wise and wonderful Athena," she thought. "It worked!"

Iole had scurried between the piles of skeletons, always keeping the eye in sight as she tried to get behind it. Approaching the wall of black mortar and bones, she crawled along its foundation for several meters. The chanting voice was close by, droning incessantly. Nearing the base of a pile of skeletons, there was suddenly a bright flash from the eye. A warm wind blew past her and she was pelted with chunks, shards, and splinters of wood. Immediately she turned her face away and threw her hands up to protect the back of her head.

Two bony hands grabbed her wrists and Iole was yanked onto her feet, her face inches away from two bulging eyes, a row of hideous yellow teeth, and tufts of matted black hair.

The only thing missing . . . was half of the flesh.

The chanting had stopped. When the dust settled there was nothing but silence in the great chamber. The eye was still there, glowing a dull white, the invisible barrier was still in place, and Pandy was still hovering high in the air. The only motion in the room was the slow spread of blood across the front of Pandy's toga.

Pandy looked all over the chamber. A sudden movement caught her eye. Two figures, one surely that of a man and the other, a tiny figure, were struggling by the back wall of bones. Pandy quickly looked to her friends, but before she could count the shapes behind the barrier, she felt herself moving through the air—over another pole.

And the chanting resumed.

Something deep within her, she could not say exactly what, gave a tiny snort, which traveled up her throat, around her brain, and shot out of her mouth.

This was ridiculous.

"I can do it again, you know!"

Quickly calculating the closest pole, she focused her mind again. From somewhere far below, she heard a shrill voice commanding something to "let go!" but deliberately ignored whatever it might be. Concentrating, she waited for the silence that would come when her powers were strongest.

And there it was. Pure quiet.

Five meters away, the top of the pole began to smoke, then glow, then flame. The pole quivered slightly, but this time, instead of a streak of fire splitting it down the center, the whole thing just exploded.

A chunk of wood shot through the great, hovering eye, causing a ripple in the light.

Her hearing returned, but there was stillness below. After a long, long pause, the light pulsed again and Pandy was moving once more.

"Okay, now I'm mad!" she shouted.

She destroyed five more poles before she realized she was floating much faster than before and the chanting was continuing throughout every blast.

"Bring it on!" she cried, exploding three more. Any pain from the wound in her stomach was pushed aside as her skill at being able to concentrate quickly was growing, shaping, and sharpening itself moment by moment.

Ten more poles shattered.

Instead of growing weary, Pandy's brain called upon all its energy reserves, diverting all thought to the task at hand.

Three more poles incinerated.

And twenty more after that.

Wood shards were flying pell-mell all over the chamber like bats suddenly exposed to sunlight.

Finally, every upright pole in the entire burial chamber had been reduced to ashes.

And still Pandy hung in midair. With nothing left to burn, her brain allowed other parts of itself to open back up. Her arms and legs now ached, feeling incredibly heavy. The pain from her wound was intense. The muscles in her back and neck were strained from being forced to bow. She was completely exhausted.

"Let go of me!" Iole yelled, trying frantically to free herself from the decaying hands. She twisted herself like a banner in a high wind, fighting the grip of the living corpse. As the first rush of hot air blasted past them, the figure glared upward at Pandora and Iole caught a snarl on the decomposing lips.

"Your power is no match for Horus," the figure muttered in a foreign tongue, his head craned back, exposing his cracked neck bones. He turned back toward Iole, baring yellow teeth.

"Her blood would have met my needs. But yours will do."

"I don't know what you're saying, you . . . you . . . fiend!" Iole said, trying to kick at the exposed shinbones and kneecaps. The corpse, still clutching her tiny wrists, lifted her off her feet and was pulling her toward its gaping jaws. Iole saw the lips parting again and realized in a panic that the creature meant to bite her!

Just then a shard of wood flew through the open mouth and into the skull where it rattled around, sounding like a musical instrument.

They were both blown backward by the force of the

next pole exploding. The corpse dropped Iole and turned to look around the chamber as one by one the thick impaling poles were being decimated.

"Bite me? I think not!" Iole said, running as fast as she could, then hiding behind a particularly large pile of bones, from which she could watch the corpse and Pandy and keep herself from being pummeled with debris.

"Why am I still up here?" Pandy thought after the dust from the last pole settled.

And then she saw it . . . in a far corner. Glinting with the light from the eye. One last pole she hadn't noticed because of its dark color. This one was made of metal—bronze, she thought, from the color of the sheen, and it was engraved with hundreds of symbols, much like the murals on the walls around her. The skeleton on it was still clothed in fine, rich fabrics and a golden, multijeweled ring hung precariously at the end of a finger.

Once more she was moved through the air. Once more she heard the chanting, only this time it was as a whisper, concentrated and fervent. Once more she summoned her will and focused, directing her power over fire at the long piece of metal.

Nothing happened. She couldn't even tell if the pole was getting warm. Except that, even though the pole was at least twenty meters ahead of her, she was aware of descending slightly. Pandy gave a quick glance at the terrible eye; the light around it flickered.

"It's weakening," she thought.

But so was she.

As the power of the eye decreased, so did its ability to suspend her in midair. If she was dropped she could be killed, but she instinctively knew that this had become a fight to the very finish.

She dropped another meter.

She turned her focus back to the bronze pole, and saw to her utter shock that the pole was beginning to shine very brightly, small rivulets of metal beginning to run down the sides. A flash made her glance at the jeweled ring, still holding fast to the bony hand, but melting now, golden drops and gems falling to the ground below.

"The heat is going through the bones," she thought.

And then she realized that something, somewhere, was totally, totally, totally . . . wrong.

There was no way she should have been able to heat the metal that quickly, if at all. She had only concentrated for a moment before she turned away to look at the eye. And she was so, so tired.

She dropped again with a jolt, the pole now only about eight meters in the distance. As she watched, the bronze completely washed away, revealing a smaller pole inside made of gold.

"Stop," she thought. "Don't think about it anymore."

She turned her thoughts away from heating the metal, shutting off her concentration entirely.

But it was too late. It was out of her control.

She was heading toward the ground, fast.

The golden pole, which even Pandy knew should have completely dissolved with such heat, was still standing upright, glowing as if lit from within.

She looked anywhere but directly at it, and tried to think about anything else: her dad and Xander and Mount Olympus and the volcano under the amphitheater back at school and the wall murals and why wasn't this gold pole melted already?

Crash!

Pandy hit the ground with a thud.

Slowly getting to her feet, she stared up at the pole, only a meter away and now glowing a brilliant sunset red. She backed up into a pile of bones, made her way around two other piles, passed the intensely flickering eye, and watched as the pole began to shake violently.

"Ahh . . . ahh . . . ," Pandy cried.

Then an otherworldly scream filled the chamber and the pole exploded into millions of pieces, raining molten gold.

A gold coating covered the closest bone piles and the walls were splattered from forty meters away. The terrible eye was so pelted that the flickering became furious until the eye finally collapsed in upon itself and disappeared altogether. The chamber was almost in complete darkness; the only light remaining was from the small fires consuming the last remnants of the wooden impaling poles.

Before the eye had flickered out, Homer caught sight of Iole, well hidden behind a bone pile. Even with the invisible wall between them, Homer had instinctively covered himself, Alcie, and Dido with his massive cloak during the explosion. Even though it had actually happened at the other end of the chamber, the force was such that a steaming golden mist traveled the entire length of the room in seconds. Instantly they were covered.

"Prunes! I guess the wall's gone," Alcie said, clinging to Homer.

"I guess."

Homer's cloak not only provided excellent protection, it also gave Alcie a chance to throw her arms once again around the youth, feeling strangely comfortable and yet uncomfortable at the same time. She silently berated herself for getting all squishy inside while her best friends were probably on their way down to the underworld.

For one moment, the explosion lit up the room as bright as day. Then Pandy felt the hot wind rush past her as the chamber was thrown into darkness. But she hadn't turned her head in time nor dived behind the bone pile quickly enough.

Flying drops of gold pelted her exposed arms and legs. Many of the pieces were, by that time, cooled enough not to do any severe damage, just glance off her skin, searing it a little.

But a piece the size of a large olive pit penetrated her left leg from behind, lodging just below the bend in her knee. Another piece, like a lemon seed, hit her right shoulder in the soft, fleshy part just under the bone. And finally, a small chunk of gold sliced through her delicate cheek, barely missing her left eye. It wedged itself just underneath her skin, like a tiny teardrop—just as luminous, and an equal symbol of pain.

CHAPTER FOURTEEN

The Corpse

6:01 p.m.

Pandy was first aware of lying on the ground feeling crunchy bits under her body; then the foul odor and the sound of several people running, stumbling, and yelling. Someone tripped over her and went crashing into a bone pile.

"This is just so wrong!"

There was the sound of someone disentangling from a mass of bones. Finally she could hear someone shouting close by. She felt a dull pain from the small wound in her stomach and a fire shot through her right shoulder.

"Ouch! Stop!"

She fully came to, realizing it was just too dark to see anything.

"What? What do I have? It's just your arm, right? I wasn't doing anything. Figs, I was just shaking you a little," said Alcie.

"I know, but there's something . . . ow! Something's

under the skin!" Pandy said, lightly touching the hard lump in her shoulder, blood trickling from the new wound.

"Why did you do that, Pandy?" Iole asked. "You could have been killed."

"It's not like I meant to," Pandy said. "I . . . it got out of control. Where are you? I can barely see anything."

"I'm right here," came Iole's voice on Pandy's right. Pandy thought she was sitting or crouching close to the floor.

"I'm here," Homer's voice hung above her.

"Alcie?" asked Pandy, swinging her arm into something solid yet soft.

"Ow . . . prunes!" Alcie said. "That was my left leg."

"Which one?" asked Iole.

"Okaaaay . . ."

"We need some light," Homer spoke up.

"Yeah," Alcie said. "Pandy, set something on fire."

"As if!" said Pandy, with a tone in her voice that put an end to the subject.

"Fine," Alcie replied, "something's still smoldering by that far wall. I'll see what I can find."

"I'll go with you," said Homer.

"No. You should stay here. If Pandy's really hurt, you're the only one who can carry her out," said Alcie, wondering what, exactly, had made her say such a self-less thing.

As Alcie moved through the darkness toward the glowing embers, Pandy tried to sit up.

"Ow! I got hit behind my knee, too. Oh, great Poseidon . . . my stomach!" she said, rubbing her sore leg, sore shoulder, and her tummy. Her scraped hip was also beginning to throb.

Dido padded over and licked her face.

"Hello, ghost dog—ow!" Her hand flew to her left cheek and she felt the open wound just below her eye. She pressed her skin slightly, feeling the lump of gold embedded in her face.

"Gods . . . this one could have taken out my eye."

"Great Zeus!" said Iole. "You've got as many holes as the sieve of the Danaides!"

"I'd laugh if it didn't hurt so much," Pandy said, then, "So you guys saw everything, right? Hey! What was that thing keeping you guys over by the entryway?"

"It was a barrier . . . a force of some kind," said Iole. "We could see everything but there was no way to get to you."

"I tried to smash it," said Homer.

"I climbed over and I was trying to get around behind that eye—which, by the way, Homer says is basically a symbol of protection and healing . . ."

"Yeah, right!" Pandy snorted.

". . . but then I was attacked by this . . ." Iole suddenly froze.

"This what, Iole?" asked Pandy.

"It was a-a . . . thing," she stammered. "A man . . . but not . . ."

Iole bolted straight up.

"Hey, I saw something too," Pandy said, "but I was too high up . . ."

"Oh no—Alcie!" Iole cried. "Oh Gods . . . where's Alcie? Alcie?"

Iole started off in the direction Alcie had gone. Homer tried hold her back but it was too late.

"I'll go after her," he said.

"Not without me," Pandy replied. "Just help me stand, okay?"

But as she took her first step on her wounded leg, she stumbled slightly. Without a word, Homer scooped Pandy up and carried her like a lamb, with Dido following at his heels.

The two raced off after Iole, trying to keep the little fires in sight. Iole quickly got lost in a dead end of bone piles, which gave Homer and Pandy enough time to catch up.

"What is it, Iole?" Pandy asked. "What did you see?"

Iole was breathing hard, the fear making it difficult for her to talk.

"It was a—"

But she cut herself off with a sharp breath, her eyes staring at the far wall.

Homer and Pandy followed her gaze.

Two large figures were silhouetted over the faded murals, lit by the glow of several small fires. Huge shadows of a girl and some type of creature grappling with each other, the girl's mouth seemingly covered by a bony claw. The creature was darting forward whenever it had the opportunity, aiming straight for the girl's neck.

"He's trying to bite her!" said Iole.

"Homer, put me down!" cried Pandy.

Without another word, the group ran at a tear toward the far wall, not caring what they crashed into or lurched over, guided only by fear.

They curved around a particularly large bone pile, and as they came into a small clearing, there was Alcie: one decaying arm encircling her waist, the other bony hand clutching her throat.

"Come no closer!"

The hand squeezed a little tighter at Alcie's throat; she struggled for air.

"Wait!" said Homer, throwing his arms out to stop Pandy and Iole from rushing forward.

No one moved for several seconds. Pandy stared at Alcie, who stared right back, eyes wide and hands trembling.

Pandy looked at Homer, about to ask what they should do next since she didn't have the faintest idea.

"Come no closer!" the corpse said again.

"What's it saying, Homer?" asked Pandy.

Suddenly, two of the corpse's fingers simply snapped off. Alcie thought her throat had been pierced, but when she realized that she could breathe a little easier, her eyes went wider as she looked from Pandy to Iole to Homer.

The corpse tried wiggling the missing fingers before it let out a terrible cry. Sagging for a moment, it then clutched Alcie even tighter.

"Just a drop," it said. "I need only a little . . . and i will have it!"

"No," said Homer quietly.

The left shinbone suddenly snapped in two; the corpse and Alcie stumbled back for a split-second before recovering their balance.

"Homer, please," Pandy cried, "just tell me what it's saying."

The corpse opened its mouth and tilted its head toward Alcie's throat, all the while keeping its eyes focused on Homer.

Homer, with the speed of a striking serpent, snatched up a large piece of wood still aflame. He moved toward the corpse, threatening it with the fire.

The corpse moved back quickly, neatly separating itself from its right foot, which stayed exactly where it was. The remaining flesh on the back of its leg dropped off the bone and plopped onto the floor. The corpse was now at an odd angle and had to readjust its hold on Alcie.

Two fingers on its right hand fell to the floor and its left eyebrow slid an inch down its face.

"By the mercy of Osiris," the corpse said, a hint of pleading in its voice, "I beg you . . . I need her living blood."

"Uh-uh," said Homer, shaking his head.

"Uh-uh?" said Iole. "You're saying uh-uh?"

Two of its exposed ribs dropped to the ground.

Homer, who had been as taut as a festival drum, let his shoulders drop. He handed the flaming brand to Pandy and walked straight up to the corpse.

The corpse tried to move, but the right thighbone fell out of its socket, and the whole upper body swung out as if it were on a hinge and several pieces of dried skin just fluttered into the air like paper.

Homer grabbed Alcie and pulled her easily out of the corpse's hold. Then, just before the corpse's entire frame went crashing to the ground, Homer deftly grabbed the skull and set it on the nearest bone pile.

For several minutes, they stood mute and staring at the skull; its two grayish eyes now clouding over with a thin opaque film.

"I think it's dead," said Iole softly.

"No, look," Alcie said.

A single red tear was slowly coursing over the bones and dried flesh of its left cheek.

Homer began to speak rapidly and low. The skull made no sound; it only stared reproachfully at the big youth, as if everything that had happened to it was somehow Homer's fault. Then slowly it opened its mouth.

Homer lifted the skull to his ear, ignoring the left eyebrow that finally slipped onto the floor, and everyone heard a faint rattling sound.

"What's that?" Pandy asked Alcie.

"Apricots, I don't know."

Iole remembered the piece of splintered wood that flew into the corpse's mouth. Now it was trapped inside the skull and it reminded her of a toy she'd played with as a child. Now, watching this afflicted thing try to speak, it was no longer amusing.

Homer and the skull began talking heatedly, with Homer every so often looking off to his left and furrowing his brow. Pandy knew it would be foolish to interrupt. She leaned against a bone pile while Alcie and Iole plopped on the ground. Dido wouldn't leave Pandy's side, refusing even to sit down.

Finally, Homer set the skull back on the bone pile.

"Come on," he said, moving quickly past the girls, "and bring your water-skins."

"Wait!" said Alcie. "We have to find them first!"

"Well, hurry," Homer said. "He doesn't have much time."

Several minutes later the girls met on the spot where Pandy had first landed, each carrying their water-skins.

"Homer?" called Pandy.

"Over here," came the reply. His huge arm waved a large burning torch, leading them toward the place where the golden pole had once stood.

Picking their way through the rubble, the girls met Homer, peering down into a well-defined pile of ashes.

"What are we looking for?" asked Pandy.

"Jewels," Homer replied. "A ruby and a sapphire. They should have landed right on top of his bones."

"They did . . . at least I think they did," Pandy said, remembering the dripping gold ring. "I watched them fall."

"Here," said Iole. Stooping, her fingers stretched toward a bright red stone. "I found the ruby."

"No!" Homer cried. "Don't touch it! It's cursed."

"Okay," said Alcie. "So what now?"

"Now we each take just a little bit of the ashes around it. We mix them with water and we drink it."

After a long moment, Alcie was the first to speak.

"You're one funny youth."

"I'm not joking. Habib—the corpse—assures me that this will work."

"What will work?" said Alcie.

"Can we at least know why?" said Pandy.

"I'll explain it later. Just trust me, okay? Since you guys don't know exactly where you're going to go on this quest, this might be useful. If it doesn't work, no big deal."

"Except I'll basically be a cannibal," said Alcie.

"Okay, fine," said Pandy finally, filling her little silver drinking cup with a small amount of water from her water-skin.

Iole and Alcie did the same and Homer, careful not to touch the ruby or the sapphire (once he found it), scooped up a tiny amount of ashes and dropped them into each girl's cup. After swirling it around, looking at each other like they were crazy, they each took a sip.

"Drink it all," said Homer.

Iole began to choke as she finished off her cup. Pandy felt as if she were going to bring it all back up again. Alcie stomped her feet in order to get her mixture down.

"Absolute nectar!" she said. "Am I right? Oh . . . oh no . . . great Zeus . . ."

Suddenly Alcie pitched forward and stumbled, landing right next to Pandy's feet and Iole, already lying on the ground. Pandy was barely able to watch Homer filling a cup with water and ashes. Then she too moaned and fell to the ground.

CHAPTER FIFTEEN

The Tale of Habit

6:23 p.m.

Millions of small lightning bolts were going off in Pandy's brain, completely blinding her. She was dizzy right up to the point of fainting, but never quite blacking out, as a sizzling sound grew louder in her ears. She rolled on the floor, unsure which way was up. Standing was out of the question—she felt as if her entire body could fly off into the heavens at any moment. She was vaguely aware that Alcie was moving around next to her, Iole was lying motionless, and Homer had caromed off a bone pile and was hunched over like an old man.

Slowly, the tiny flashes began to dissipate, and darkness was taking over. She lay panting, exhausted again, and once more aware of the throbbing pain in various parts of her body.

Alcie reached over and grabbed her arm, trying to sit up.

"I'll kill him!" she said, flailing with her other arm in Homer's general direction.

Iole's eyes fluttered open.

"I now know what it's like to die."

"Homer! You mind telling us what just happened?" said Pandy.

Homer was leaning against a bone pile, his barrel chest heaving wildly, staring at the girls.

"Here goes," Pandy heard him say, then . . .

"You guys should be able to understand everything I'm saying even though I'm talking . . . like . . . in a totally different language."

"Yeah," said Alcie, "so what? Of course we can understand you . . ."

Alcie was suddenly silent. Pandy saw Homer's mouth forming oddly shaped words; she knew in her head she shouldn't be able to understand anything he was saying and yet it was all as clear as pure water in a shallow bowl.

"Homer," said Pandy, "say it again."

"Can you guys understand me?"

"Yes!" Pandy cried. "Yes! I can totally understand you!"

Her hand flew to her mouth.

"I understand him!" said Iole.

"Me too," Alcie replied.

"How were you able to understand the corpse in the first place?" asked Pandy.

"Gladiator school. Easy Egyptian."

"Homer, say something else," Pandy asked.

"No time," Homer said, charging forward through the bone piles. "We gotta get back."

But as he wound his way toward the skull again, he called back a few of the simple phrases he had learned in gladiator school: phrases in basic Sumerian, Ethiopian, and Latin. Pandy, Alcie, and Iole understood every word.

"I don't believe this," Pandy said as they stood once more around the living skull. "How did drinking that stuff make us able to understand?"

"Okay . . . like . . . what happened is . . . ," Homer began.

"It is simple, if you will listen," said the skull, its eyes fast losing their luster. "But you must be very quiet; my time is almost at an end."

The eyes rolled in their sockets as a few old eyelashes fell out and a hunk of brittle hair dropped off to one side. The ancient tongue, it seemed, suddenly went very dry.

"You drank in the bones of Calchas, an influential adviser to a great pharaoh. He was a master of languages in his native Greece and, as such, the Greek general, Agamemnon, sought his wisdom and ability to translate documents before Agamemnon decided to invade the city of Troy. But Calchas translated something incorrectly and so the Greeks lost many men in the Trojan War. Calchas was to be executed, but he escaped here to Egypt and became the confidant of the pharaoh."

"However, Calchas soon developed an insatiable thirst for power and began to learn the arts of magic and enchantments. He became so skilled that many thought him to be as powerful as any of our gods. He sought to assassinate the pharaoh and assume the throne for himself, but was stopped just in time. He was impaled on a gold and bronze pole from which his spirit could never rise. The priests of the pharaoh cursed his soul, imprisoning it in the ruby and sapphire of his ring. Touching the stones would have immediately brought his soul back to the land of the dead from the darkness that holds it. Now, it is trapped forever."

"But how did drinking his bone . . . dust help us to understand?" asked Pandy.

"He felt so sure that he would rise again and regain his former shape before the flesh left his bones that he mocked the priests and left a taunt: the ability to know all languages if anyone was clever enough to crush his bones and ingest them."

"How did you know this?" asked Pandy.

"The slaves who carried him here spoke of it as they

stood the bronze pole on its end. Naturally, they were all put to death for learning of the curse."

"Naturally," said Iole.

"Why did you tell us what to do?" Pandy asked the skull.

"Yeah . . . before, you wanted to eat me. Now you're helping us?" said Alcie. "Why?"

"The boy wanted to know why I needed your . . . blood."

"But I was having trouble with some of the big words in Egyptian," said Homer, looking off.

"As I said, I don't have much time left," the skull added. "So I told him what to do. He obviously thought you all would benefit."

"It's just that they laugh at me when I know stuff . . . ," Homer complained under his breath.

"All right," said Pandy, looking at Homer.

"Sheesh!" said Alcie.

Pandy turned back to the skull. "I would like to know why you need our blood."

"My own curse," said the skull. "But my story is simple. My name was Habib and I was a common bricklayer, working on the tomb of the great Tutankhamen. I stole an amulet, a symbol of the Eye of Horus, that had been blessed and left in the tomb for Tutankhamen to find after his death. The amulet was to heal any wounds to the pharaoh's body as it made its journey to Osiris and the land of shadows. I knew that the priest's blessing made it very valuable and it would bring a high price if I could sell it. But I was caught coming out of the tomb and condemned to death."

"By impaling?" asked Pandy.

The skull of Habib looked at Pandy with what little surprise it could muster, sending the right eyebrow sliding down over the nose cavity.

"Of course. You know another way?"

"Figs."

"Please, go on," said Iole.

"I was executed two days later," the skull continued slowly. "But unknown to anyone, including me, was that the chain and the Eye of Horus had fallen into my waistcloth and was pressed against my skin. It was still on my body when I was brought into this chamber. So I was not truly dead. My body decayed, but the healing eye amulet with its blessing has kept me alive for centuries. Enough years to see to hundreds of people interred here, including Calchas. My flesh is almost gone, but my tormented spirit has lived."

"Let's get to the part with the blood," said Alcie.

"Whenever a life force entered the chamber, a priest, a slave, a mourner, anyone, the eye would try to heal and restore me by enabling me to kill him and drink his blood. The force would impale him, but at his moment of death, his blood was no longer useful. It's the reason that this temple was abandoned: stories of the monster in the Chamber of Despair and the certain death that awaited anyone in here."

"If it's keeping you alive, why did your bones crack and break just now?" asked Pandy.

"Everything must turn to dust eventually," replied the skull. "No matter that my soul will live on, this is the moment of my final physical death. I even doubt that drinking blood would have really helped at this point."

The skull's tongue swelled up then shriveled again, turning darker by the second. It turned its sad, rheumy eyes on Pandy.

"The boy has briefly told me of your quest. Your powers must be great indeed, young one, to have done the things that I witnessed in this chamber."

It paused for a moment, then with great effort spoke again.

"I do not know if it will help, but I would like you to take the Eye of Horus. It is the only thing I have and it was never really mine to begin with. Use it as you can. Perhaps . . . by passing it to worthier hands, the great Nephthys and Osiris will pity me and allow me into the land of the dead. It is the only thing I can do."

"Thank you," Pandy said, watching as the light in its eyes began to fade away.

"It is there, wound around my rib bones, underneath

that bit of cloth," said the skull, gazing in the direction of his shattered skeleton.

Pandy walked to the pile of bones and peeled away the centuries-old gauze covering the tiny floating rib at the bottom. There, a thin gold chain and a miniature golden eye the size of a green olive glinted in the dying firelight. Holding it in her hands, she approached the skull again.

"Thank you," she repeated.

"Wear it and you may be surprised," said the skull, coughing softly. Then, in a whisper, it said, "The people pray where you come from, don't they?"

"Of course," said Pandy.

"Then, perhaps, you might say one for me. You seem to be important. Someone important might listen."

Pandy walked up to the skull and bent down very close.

"I will. I promise."

And the last of the light in its eyes went out.

No one said anything for a while. Finally, Homer said, "How long do you think we've been in here?"

"An hour, at least," said Iole, straightening herself. "The sun's probably set."

"Great, out of the dark and into the dark," said Alcie.

"Well, at least the air will be fresh. Come on," said Pandy, tightening the small clasp on the chain and settling the eye onto her neck. She wasn't certain but she thought the pain of her many wounds lessened in that instant. Picking up a small piece of wood still alight with flame, she led them back across the chamber toward the entryway.

At the opening, Pandy turned around.

"What?" said Alcie.

Pandy gazed at the pole shards, the huge murals on the walls, the terrible piles of bones disappearing into blackness. For a second she thought that nothing Hera could conjure up could ever be as bad as this chamber. Then she almost laughed out loud—this room would be a child's playroom to Hera.

"Pandy?" said Iole.

"Huh? Oh. Yeah, I'm okay. Let's get out of here."

As they trudged up the gentle incline toward the surface, the air was indeed fresher with each step and the light was growing brighter.

"Good," said Homer, "sun's still up. Maybe we'll find a nice spot to camp."

"Camp?" sputtered Alcie, as they neared the opening onto the temple terrace. "Sorry, but I'm not leaving this temple tonight. It's covered . . . except where the roof has fallen in. It's kinda protected . . . except where the walls have caved."

"We should try to make up some time . . . ," Iole began.

"But best of all, since this place is known to be so . . .

like . . . haunted," Alcie continued, following Pandy onto the terrace and into the setting afternoon sun, "there won't be anyone around to mess with us."

She put her hands on her hips, as if to say "and that is that!"

At that moment, across the large open terrace, forty-seven pairs of eyes saw three girls, one large youth, and a snow white dog emerge from the burial chamber beneath the temple, dirty and bloody, togas askew and hair wildly mussed.

And forty-seven mouths opened in unison to let out the most terrifying scream.

CHAPTER SIXTEEN

Into the Light

6:47 p.m.

Only one person actually threw something, as far as Pandy could tell in all the confusion and noise. A candied orange rind, aimed with no precision whatsoever, caught Pandy on the left side of her face, right on the spot where the golden shrapnel teardrop was embedded under her eye, causing it to bleed again for a few seconds.

But the ancient Chinese woman who threw it was now fleeing off the terrace and down onto the desert, along with almost everybody else.

Seconds later, the terrace of the temple was empty.

Pandy, Alcie, Iole, and Homer ran to the edge and stared down.

"Wait! Please," cried Pandy, stepping forward, listening to the panicked cries and whispers below.

In a split second, Pandy took in the entire scene: men, women, youths, maidens, a few children, and one woman clutching an infant. None of them bore any resemblance to each other, or to any people Pandy had ever seen in her life, dressed in clothing of bizarre cuts and mismatched colors.

"Who are they?" asked Alcie, quietly.

"They're the people you said wouldn't be around to mess with us," said Iole.

"Hello. My name is . . . ," Pandy began, but her voice trailed off.

A soft jangling sound began from somewhere in the crowd. Pandy could see nothing for a second, then people began to make way for a solitary figure moving steadily through the group. Something about the gait was masculine, yet the person was dressed in a long, dark robe a woman would use when visiting the baths, and a single braid of black hair looped over both shoulders. The face was impossible to read through the wrinkles. In each hand the figure held a ribbon with coins or small metal discs sewn onto it, softly shaking them with every step. Dido gave one short bark then promptly hid behind Pandy's legs.

"What sort of spirit are you?" the figure asked in high-pitched Cantonese, slowly ascending the steps to the terrace.

"I'm not a spirit," she immediately replied, pausing in her mind to roll around the short, sharp sounds of the Chinese language she'd just uttered. "Gods," Pandy thought. Drinking the ashes of Calchas not only allowed her to speak any language, but also since Calchas knew *what* each language was, that information must now be passed on to her!

"It's Chinese," Pandy heard Iole say to Alcie.

"Duh!"

The sun, hanging very low in the sky, had begun to create shadows all over the terrace and the desert below.

"Then which among you is the spirit?"

"What do you mean?" Pandy replied, now certain that the figure was an incredibly old man.

"I will banish the spirit you brought forth from the tomb, but it's been some time since I have been troubled by such foolishness and I do not want to choose the wrong one. Tell me, which is the spirit and what sort?"

As he spoke, he moved into the fading sunlight. Pandy had never seen such a face: hundreds of fine wrinkles covered every centimeter. The nose was so small as to almost not be there and the mouth had somehow been pinched so tight that the lips had disappeared. Pandy couldn't see the mouth move when he spoke.

"Tell me quickly, before the spirit jumps into one of my people."

Then Pandy realized his mouth wasn't moving at all.

As she hesitated, thinking her brain was extremely tired, the man began to jangle the coins much louder.

"I see you will not tell me. Selfish, selfish. Very well, little fish, I will banish you all to the Yangtze River and all souls will share in the exile of the evil one!"

The man opened his mouth, revealing teeth that had been filed into sharp points, and inhaled a huge breath.

Alcie stepped forward, standing directly in front of the old man.

"You're not banishing anyone, anywhere—especially Pandy! If you try it, you're gonna have to go through me!" she cried in Cantonese.

"Wait!" shouted Pandy. "None of us are evil. I just told you, we're not spirits!"

The man ceased his jangling, turning his head to look at each of the group.

"You came from beneath the temple," he thought-said.

"How's he doing that?" Alcie asked over her shoulder, still confronting the man.

"No idea," Iole said.

Pandy instantly realized the problem.

"Okay, okay, I know we came out of there," Pandy said, pointing to the entrance to the burial chamber. "But I was only in there because I fell through a trap in the desert. And they"—she gestured to Alcie, Iole, and Homer—"were only there because they came in to find me. We are not part of the curse of this temple. We're just trying to get to Alexandria, sir. And we got a little . . . lost."

"Sir," said Alcie, backing away.

"That's correct, sir," said Iole.

"Sir," said Alcie again.

The man simply looked at them for several minutes. Then he looked at the entrance to the burial chamber, then out toward the Nile, then back to his people, who had remained silent the entire time.

"Our animals are tired," he began, his mouth not moving at all. "And I'm tired. And my mother is very tired. You're lucky we stopped. We shall find you sleeping quarters and you are welcome to eat with us in the main tent, but don't go poking your noses into anything else, little fishes."

He turned and descended the steps leading down to the desert. Suddenly, the ancient Chinese woman raced past him, her voice raised in a yell, ready to hurl handfuls of candied orange rinds.

"Mother!" the man looked at the old woman. "Calm yourself. Put the oranges back into the reading jar."

He glanced back over his shoulder.

"Tell Ng to prepare something out of the ordinary. We're having little fishes for our evening meal."

His laughter could be heard as he walked into the desert, followed by the old woman who, craning her neck, never took her eyes off of Pandy, Homer, Alcie, Iole, and Dido.

CHAPTER SEVENTEEN

Campsite

7:00 p.m. (exactly)

"Alcie," Iole said, "that's a couple of times now you've put yourself between one of us and something dangerous."

"Right," Alcie replied, moving toward the terrace steps. "And your point would be? Pom-OH-granates! Great Apollo!"

Pandy, Iole, and Homer joined Alcie standing on the top step, transfixed by the sight below.

In the shadow of the temple, a dozen or so large tents had been erected in what could only have been a few hours. They were arranged in a circle around several large black wagons and a very crude makeshift corral holding many odd-looking animals: abnormally large horses, goats with horns twice their own body length, beasts that resembled both horses and dogs at once with big humps on their backs, several cages full of enormous cats of varying bright colors, one cage holding a red snake, two cages full of hummingbirds, and one empty cage of ornately carved ivory.

Now that any danger had obviously passed, people ran, strolled, and sat between the tents; many gazed warily at the group still on the temple terrace.

But it was the tents themselves that were most intriguing, and even though night was swiftly falling, Pandy could see everything clearly because lamps were being lit, illuminating everything from within.

Each tent was a different color and shape, but nothing so common as red or yellow, square or round. One tent looked just like a pistachio nut, another had all the intricate shadings of a fresh peach and resembled a floor pillow, including gigantic tassels at each corner; still another, shaped like a staircase, was the color of a blue sky at sunrise: clouds, rays of sun, and all. One tent, in the form and coloring of a mountain, had smoke, ash, and sparks—and a delicious aroma—billowing up and out of a hole in its top. Pandy saw tents shaped like a jar, a human foot, a head of garlic, and a pink and white seashell. And one, almost invisible in the growing dark, was in the shape and color of . . . a slug. She also thought this last one might actually be moving.

Pandy could tell immediately which tent belonged to the old man, not only because she saw him enter it, but because it was by far the largest and brightest; a giant tangerine tent with several crimson and lemon-colored banners fluttering high above each, bearing the initials WCL in beautiful Chinese calligraphy.

As they descended to the desert, a young girl, perhaps three or four years older than Pandy, wearing a head-dress of brilliant feathery plumes approached the group.

"Why do they have to stay in *my* tent?" Pandy heard the girl mutter as she drew closer.

She stared at Pandy with her brown almond-shaped eyes.

"I know you little girls can't understand me . . . ," she began haughtily in her native Mayan.

"Every word," said Pandy.

The girl stopped short, her mouth open. A full five seconds later, during which Alcie just grinned at her, she began again in a slightly softer tone.

"I am called Usumacinta, for the great river of my people, and I descend directly from the Wizard of the Fatal Laugh, first of the created and formed men. You will all share my tent tonight . . . except for you," she said, looking to Homer. "You will sleep at the opening to protect your women."

She turned her back and strode across the campsite toward the blue, purple, and white tent shaped like the head of garlic.

Pandy was looking at Alcie.

"Nope," Alcie said. "I'm too tired to have anything to say to that. But I'm thinking a few things."

"Doesn't she want to know who we are?" asked Pandy, following in Usumacinta's footsteps.

"We're not dangerous. I don't think she or her people could care in the slightest," Iole said.

"Everyone seems to have 'people,'" Homer mused.

"We have 'people,'" said Iole.

"Right now, we have us," said Pandy.

As they passed groups of people all talking at once about them, so many different languages came rushing in upon Pandy's head that it began to throb. As they reached the entrance to Usumacinta's tent, they each were slightly glassy-eyed from processing so many new sounds.

"Homer, could you keep Dido out here?" Pandy said. "We'll stow our stuff and then we'll go to the main tent for evening meal."

"Like . . . take your time."

He dropped to the ground, resting against one of the tent's support poles. No one noticed his eyelids slamming shut or heard the beginnings of a soft snore.

"By the way, there's one group of people speaking Abyssinian that think we're gods," said Iole, stepping into the tent.

"Yeah, well two hairy guys speaking a Norse dialect want us hung by our toes," said Pandy.

"So it evens out," said Alcie.

The tent was much roomier inside than it had

appeared. It was filled with ornate, blocky wooden carvings, simple brass oil lamps, a metal rack from which hung several heavy-looking feathered dresses, and about ten large green birds perched on a carved wooden tree. A huge hammock had been strung from one support pole to another, heavily laden with silk and cotton cushions. Three sleeping pallets were being hastily made up by two of the most grotesque creatures Pandy had ever seen. One had a mouth that covered the entire bottom half of her face and was making a sort of sucking sound, and the other had two extra bumps on her shoulders, almost like two extra necks, and a mouth full of three separate rows of teeth.

"Thank you, Scylla. Thank you, Charybdis," said Usumacinta, in halting, broken Greek. The two women finished and stood up, nodding their heads furiously, but as neither of them spoke Mayan, Scylla started making wide, scrubbing gestures, sending Alcie into hysterics, and Charybdis began a little dance, uttering a few words.

"Wait!" Pandy cried. "We're Greek!"

The conversation that followed (they decided to escort the girls to the bathing tent the following morning) took only a few seconds and left Usumacinta completely bewildered. Scylla and Charybdis left, chattering away about "such nice Greek girls." Pandy chose a sleeping pallet and stowed her pouch and water-skin underneath. She hesitated a moment before unlacing her sandals and removing her mother's silver girdle, pausing as she undid the clasps. How much older she felt with the girdle on! Now looking at it lying on the pallet, Pandy felt just a twinge of her own inadequate thirteen-year-old self again. All at once, her heart gave an involuntary shudder—she wanted nothing more in the world at that moment than to see her mother again. Because, she realized, taking in a sharp breath of fear, she couldn't exactly recall her mother's face. Then, suddenly, she felt nothing but tired.

"Hey, guys, I'm just gonna lie down and shut my eyes for a sec . . . ," she began, turning around to the others. Usumacinta was standing in the middle of her tent, looking back and forth between Alcie and Iole, both passed out cold on their pallets.

Smiling, Pandy told herself she would wake them in a few moments when she roused herself, then she lay down, closing her eyes.

The next instant, the face of Morpheus, God of Dreams, appeared before her.

"Hello again, Pandora."

"Hi, Morpheus," her mind answered.

"Quite a day for you."

"Yep."

"You haven't eaten much of anything, you know."

"I don't care," she said.

"You may wake up with a stomachache," he persisted.

"That's okay, I'm good. I'm just so tired."

"Very well then, off you go," he said, and Pandy felt him envelop her mind.

"Thank you," she managed.

"My pleasure. Dream . . . of nothing."

And she was gone.

CHAPTER EIGHTEEN

Just a Little Chat

7:16 p.m.

"Dear, precious child," Hera said to herself. "Precious, darling, resourceful, intrepid, sensible, cunning, conniving, presumptuous, arrogant brat of a child!"

She pounded her large fist into a rose-colored silk pillow, sprawling on the divan in her spacious suite of rooms. Before her stood an elaborate, many-armed candelabra, a wax taper ablaze in each sconce. When lit, each flame showed a tiny portion of whatever view or scene Hera wished to see at any given moment. Right now, her beautiful but bulging eyeballs were trained on a garlic-shaped tent in the Egyptian desert, and the three sleeping girls inside.

"Just how clever do you really think you are, Pandora?" she mused. "Surely even you must realize that the only thing keeping me from dropping you headfirst off the slopes of Olympus or turning you into a grain of sand—or into my hairbrush, for that matter—

is the fact that my husband would be slightly miffed at me."

Hera knew (much) better; Zeus would stick her head-down in a frozen Norse lake if he even *suspected* she was interfering with Pandy's quest. All her plans were riding on her ability to be subtle (not one of Hera's strong suits). And time.

"Why oh why couldn't you cooperate and simply have been skewered on a pole in that dreadful tomb? Ah, me," she exhaled heavily. "Patience is all I need. And if I can just figure out how to cultivate that . . ."

She poked a large forefinger into one of the small flames in the candelabra showing Pandy's tummy. On her cot, Pandy moaned in her sleep while dreaming about her stomach being attacked by enormous rodents.

"I have it!" came a loud whisper.

Demeter swept in, breathless, flushed, and rather giggly; her hair changing seasons very quickly in her excitement.

"Excellent!" said Hera, blowing out the candles. "Give it to me."

From her robes, Demeter withdrew a small clay jar. Hera snatched it with one hand while she cleared her admiring table (as she called it) of all its pots, brushes, and creams with the other.

"Come," she called, summoning two deep chairs from across the room. "This should be interesting."

"Oh, I'm all peppery and speckled inside!" Demeter began, giving her hands a little shake. "You have no idea . . . Just a little *chat* with Zeus, you said? The moment I mentioned what a shame it was that since he'd been forced to reduce Pandora's mother to ashes and he's had no chief personal aide in his Athens temple since, he got all pouty. And that's when, just as you predicted, Hera, he sort of wandered over to his table and gently touched that jar. So that's when I knew which one she was in."

"How did you distract him long enough to steal it?" asked Hera, regarding the jar from underneath her alternately arching brows.

"I looked out the window and told him I thought I saw that pretty Greek maiden, Atalanta, jogging on the beach. I turned around and he was gone."

"Yes," Hera sighed, "my husband likes girls who run. Of course, they're usually running away from him."

"He should be gone for a while. So . . ."

Demeter sat down and stared at Hera like she was about to see the earth created before her eyes.

With a wave, Hera removed the wax seal and lid from the jar. Turning it over, she spilled the little heap of ashes into her hand. With a giant breath she blew them toward her mirror. In a direct line they flew, passing through the leaded glass and into the identical room on the other side. The ashes swirled in the mirror image, spinning quickly at first, then slowly condensing and compacting themselves into the form of a statuesque and beautiful woman . . . albeit missing a right arm.

"Hera!" said Demeter.

"Oops," Hera said. "Hang on, for my sake." She picked up a few unblown ashes from her palm and threw them at the mirror. After swirling furiously for a few seconds they settled into Sybilline's lovely right arm.

"Thank you. Hello? Excuse me," came Sybilline's small, tinny voice through the glass.

"All right, Pandora's mother," said Hera, settling herself in a chair. "What I basically need to know is this: what is it that really matters most to your daughter?"

"I'm sorry," Sybilline looked around her and became a little frantic, "but I'm not quite sure where I am."

Hera hung her head and gave an exasperated sigh.

"You can't really blame her, Hera," said Demeter softly. "She's been ashes for over a month."

"Wife of Prometheus," said Hera, "I understand your confusion and I shall put your fears to rest."

With another wave of Hera's hand, Sybilline visibly relaxed. She stood placidly, gazing at the two goddesses with a small half smile on her face.

"Answer, do not ask. Do you understand?" asked Hera.

"Yes, great one."

"Oh, that's nice," said Demeter. "You're so good with people."

"Thank you, I try. Now, mother of Pandora, tell me, what is it that matters most to your daughter?"

Sybilline stood still on the other side. Staring.

"You didn't by accident make her deaf, did you?" asked Demeter.

"I don't think so," said Hera. "Mother of Pandora, what is it that your daughter values most highly?"

Suddenly, Sybilline thrust one hip ever so slightly forward and crossed her arms.

"I have no idea."

"What?" said Hera.

"I'm just trying to think. She's very curious, many things interest her. But something special? No. I don't really know."

"A mother not knowing what her daughter likes and loves? Her tastes? Her preferences?" said Demeter. "That's not right. That's just not right!"

"I'm stunned and, being the protectoress of mothers," said Hera, "I should and would punish you . . . if this were anyone but Pandora we were talking about. But time is short. Come now, you can't think of anything that she wants, needs, dotes upon, and so on?"

"She has two friends she's always talking about," replied Sybilline.

"Alcie and Iole, yes, we know," said Hera.

"And there was a boy she was interested in," Sybilline continued.

"Tiresias the Younger was turned into a girl when the box was opened, so he's out of the picture," said Hera.

"There is only one other thing I can think of. Actually, I don't know why I didn't think of it before. The one thing Pandora truly loves is Dido," said Sybilline.

"Dido?"

"Her dog," said Sybilline.

Hera had a short, sharp intake of breath. Then, after a long pause, she exhaled very, very slowly, never for a moment taking her eyes off Sybilline.

She waved her hand one final time and a very surprised Sybilline watched as fragments of her body began whirling in the space around her, until she was nothing but a swirling circle of ashes. Hera sucked a large breath of air inward and the ashes flew out of the mirror image and back into the clay jar. Hera placed the lid on the jar herself and gazed at Demeter's reflection in her looking glass.

Turning to her friend, Hera's lips began spreading over her teeth at hideous, malevolent angles.

"Of course. It was there all the time. The girl loves her dog!"

CHAPTER NINETEEN

Sentry

7:00 p.m. (exactly . . . the next day)

"Humpf . . . Dido, stop!" In her sleep, Pandy swatted at something close to her ear. "Stop . . . um . . . big . . . thing . . . you're tickling me!" Still foggy, Pandy opened her eyes and saw Dido sitting on his haunches a meter away, just staring at her.

"Stop it, ghost dog, stop kissing me. Uh . . . huh?" Pandy reached toward her ear and felt a tiny tongue, a small warm snout, and a big hunk of fur.

"Ahh!" she screamed, grabbing whatever it was and sending it hurtling across the tent. Dido watched the little missile arc overhead and padded off to the spot where it had landed with a thud.

Pandy bolted up too quickly, saw a zillion stars swirling before her eyes, and promptly fell back on the pallet.

"Great Artemis!" she moaned.

"How interesting you should mention her," came a

small, raspy voice close by. "I mean, of all the goddesses, I just find it fascinating that you would choose her . . . seeing as how she gave me to you, seeing as how the Huntress and I are so close. She and I."

Dido stood directly in front of her, her wolfskin diary held loosely in his mouth. The diary gave a few low grunts and growls and Dido very gently shook the skin back and forth, causing much dust to fly into the air. Then he carefully placed it on the pallet next to Pandora.

The diary gave a small yelp. Dido yelped in response then settled himself back on the floor.

"Oh, forgive me, Pandora. I was just thanking your dog for dusting me off . . . after retrieving me from the dirt floor . . . in that filthy corner . . . where you threw me!"

"I'm sorry, Diary," Pandy said, sincerely. "I didn't know that was you."

"Yes, well, someone or something had to wake you," said the diary. "Your friends decided to let you sleep, but that strange girl who lives in this place poked you a few times when meals were being served. A lot of good that did. I have been listening to your stomach growl for many hours, so finally I had Dido place me on top of your head. Thanks be to Artemis that I am only slightly bruised for my trouble."

"I'm sorry," Pandy said again in earnest. Then, without

warning, she found herself in a panic. She dropped to the floor and began pulling out her bags and pouches. "How long have I been asleep? What am I doing? What day is it? We can't stay here! I have to get to Alexandria!"

"Pandora, cease!" said the diary. "You have been keeping company with Morpheus a single day. That is all."

"But one day might make all the difference! Vanity is out there somewhere and—"

"And what can be done now? It is done. It is past," said the diary.

"I know, but—"

"Would you cross the great desert tonight, on foot, risking, perhaps, everything by being rash and unthinking?" the diary continued. "Or would you look upon and listen to what is about you?"

"What do you mean?"

"Artemis, the Huntress, tells you that there are interesting forces at work in this place. You must be keen and receptive. Use that curiosity of yours. Hunt, Pandora. Perhaps you will discover a way to expedite your journey."

"Expedite?"

"Speed up!"

"Oh!" said Pandy. "I will. I promise. Please tell Artemis."

"She heard you."

"Okay," said Pandy. Looking about, she half expected

to see Artemis floating in the air above her. Her gaze landed on her dog. "Has Dido been fed?"

"He's fine. That incredibly large boy has taken good care of him."

"Gods!" Pandy said, hearing her stomach growl. "I'm starving."

The wolfskin's large ears twitched toward the opening of the tent.

"Judging from the sound coming from thirty-seven and six-tenths paces due northeast, tonight's feast is just now under way. I'd try to dress appropriately if I were you. And fix your hair."

"Thanks for waking me," Pandy said, donning her spare toga and repinning her hair combs.

"Fine . . . have fun. Don't worry about me. I'm sure I'll hear all about it—and the temple, and the dolphins, whatever you've been doing to keep yourself busy, et cetera—later. If you can spare the time to talk to me."

"Of course. I'll tell you everything," Pandy said, kissing the little snout and carefully placing the skin back into her pouch.

"I think it would be quite nice if I could eat something," came the diary's muffled voice from under the pallet. "I never get to go anywhere!"

Smiling as she clasped her silver girdle around her waist, she left the tent.

She didn't have to get her bearings by the fading

sunset to know which way was due northeast. There was only one tent aglow with light, sound, and scent: the giant tangerine.

Making her way, all her senses were on alert to discover these "interesting forces" the diary had mentioned. She looked at everything, the tents, the animals, the crumbling temple, and the unending desert. She inhaled the twilight air, taking in deep breaths. She tried to listen more intently to every sound; to feel anything different in the air on her skin.

Nothing out of the ordinary.

Except she was miles from home and walking toward a big tangerine.

A large shadow suddenly obscured the little remaining sun and she heard a soft dragging noise directly behind her. Turning around, she saw a wall of sweating gray matter about ten meters long and almost four meters high moving slowly in a circle from the left. At the front, she saw two small protrusions, bulbous and twisting gently, like soft feelers sticking up, ready to sense any danger. It was the slug tent. Standing transfixed at the wide slime trail it was leaving behind, a sudden movement caught her eye. Cries and shouts erupted from within, and the wet slug "skin" seemed as if it was being poked with something sharp within its belly. Suddenly, it was as if a lamp had been lit inside, and the "skin" became translucent. Pandy saw several people silhouetted inside, jumping over tables, pallets, and chairs and grabbing curved items hanging on the inner walls, all headed toward the back end. Pandy could see a rickety spiral staircase loaded with everyone trying to get up and out. A small flap opened on top of the slug and five older youths, their heads wrapped in large cloth turbans and wearing flowing robes, leaped out into the darkening night air. Each of them had a bluish glow, as if they were covered head to toe in a glittery blue powder.

"Shahriyar, front! You're the main lookout tonight," shouted one man in Arabic, waving an enormous curved sword.

"Sir!"

The man called Shahriyar, brandishing his own curved weapon, ran toward the head of the slug, settling himself between the two soft horns.

"Haifz, left. Wakim, right," said the first man, obviously in charge. "Musa and I are rear."

"Wise is Abdul-Rashid al Ahmed!" shouted the men as they took their places.

"Praise be, there will be no disturbances this night," Musa said to Abdul-Rashid, seating themselves on the back end of the slug tent. "The performers are still a little . . . disturbed . . . by yesterday's arrival of our 'guests.' "

"If Wang Chun Lo is to be believed, and he always is," began Abdul-Rashid, squinting in the last of the sunlight, "they are indeed simply three girls, a boy, and a white dog. Flesh and blood, nothing more. He announced this morning that he would hear their tale tonight. But he assures us all that there is absolutely nothing to fear."

"Hello!" Pandy shouted up in flawless Arabic.

Musa screamed and Abdul-Rashid fell off the slug.

"Stay back!" cried Abdul-Rashid, leaping to his feet, then crashing backward on his bottom as his feet slipped on the shiny slime trail. "Back, I say!"

"I'm sorry," said Pandy, instinctively moving forward to help and trying not to giggle.

"No!" cried Abdul-Rashid, "do not cross the trail! It is fully charged. A very strong current. You would be killed instantly! Even though you are a woman and therefore unimportant, you are still the guest of Wang Chun Lo."

Pandy stopped laughing. Had she heard him clearly—unimportant?

"Then how can you stand . . . ?" Pandy pointed to his feet, covered in slime.

"We are the renowned Caliphs! 'Channels of Earthly Displeasure.' Night sentry for Wang Chun Lo. The slime is our creation," Musa shouted. "You've heard of us, certainly!"

"No," Pandy replied, "I haven't."

"Well, surely you have heard of Wang Chun Lo's Caravan of Wonders in whatever mud hut village you live in," scoffed Abdul-Rashid.

Pandy bristled slightly.

"I live in Athens," she replied coolly. "It's the center of the known world, and no, I've never heard of it."

"Oh, Athens. Haifz?" cried Musa over his shoulder. "When do we play Athens?"

"Five weeks," came the answer.

"Perhaps you'll see a performance then?" said Musa.

"Somehow, I don't think so," said Pandy.

Suddenly, at Abdul-Rashid's feet, there was a blue flash and a split-second buzzing ending with a tiny pop. He picked up a large blackened beetle that had crawled into the slime trail, now quite dead, smoke curling gently off its body. He examined the bug in the growing moonlight and, after inhaling deeply, took a serious bite off of one end.

"Ah, well," sneered Abdul-Rashid, walking toward the rear end of the slug, chomping on the beetle. "The great ones where you come from obviously don't think much of you to have kept our glory a secret. I would tell you all about us, but you're only a woman and we're on duty."

"Look," Pandy said, backing away from the slime trail. "I just wanted to say that we're not—my friends and I—we're not anything bad . . . we're mortal. You know, just in case you were worried."

Abdul-Rashid was attempting mad dashes up the slug's slippery tail with Musa trying to pull his captain up.

"Worried?" he panted. "I laugh at you and what you say!"

"The feast is that way!" Musa shouted, finally pulling Abdul-Rashid on top but also accidentally plucking the turban off his captain's head.

"Thank you. Um, sorry . . . again," Pandy called. She turned around, but not before hearing Abdul-Rashid ranting that, now that a female other than his wife had seen his hair, he would naturally have to shave his head.

Passing several tents, Pandy realized that the tangerine tent was silent; the earlier chatter and laughter had ceased while she had been talking to the strange sentry. In a far corner of the tent there was a loud crash, then much shushing in many languages. Then silence again. But it was the kind of silence that occurs when hearts are beating, mouths are breathing, and ears are listening—very hard.

Pandy lifted the flap of the tangerine tent and crossed over the threshold.

The interior of the tent was a riotous jumble of intricate rugs, huge floor pillows, and silk swaths crisscrossing from one tent pole to another—all in every shade of orange imaginable. Everything was either completely or mostly orange, except for some of the wilder animal-skin pillows, the bronze oil lamps, and the low-slung wooden tables dotting the room.

People were sitting on single cushions or had

stacked large bolsters to form long, low couches. The little tables were heavy with foods the likes of which Pandy had never seen.

But no one turned to look at her. Not Scylla or Charybdis, sitting together. Not even Usumacinta, who sat with a green parrot on one shoulder. No one even noticed she was there. Some people, their mouths full of food, had simply stopped chewing. Those who looked like they might be servants were standing with their arms full of steaming platters or dirty plates. Someone was in midpour of a tall teapot. Every so often a person in the crowd whispered a few words, but every eye was fixed on someone at the far end of the tent.

Someone with curly brown hair, two left feet, and a big, big mouth.

CHAPTER TWENTY

Feast

7:26 p.m.

"So that brings us up to . . . where? Figs. Oh, yeah. Okay, so we get off the dolphins and walk out into the desert. Of course, I wanted to head right to Alexandria, but Pandy needed to get her bearings and she was a little tired."

Alcie had complete command of the room, speaking in perfect Cantonese, and she was talking fast. Seated like a sultana around a wooden table, she had Iole and Homer to her right and the old man and his ancient mother on her left. Homer was gaping at Alcie, his eyebrows knit together to form one long blond line across his forehead. Iole was sitting cross-legged on what looked like a large persimmon, her elbows on her knees and her head in her hands, staring out over the crowd with a look of abject mortification.

"And then . . . like . . . all of a sudden Pandy was gone. Just disappeared. Right, Iole?"

"Oh, Alcie, you're doing such a wonderful job of telling this, you just go right ahead." Then Iole lowered her voice. "You realize you've gone nuts, right?"

"Okay, anyway . . . Pandy is just *gone*. And naturally I'm thinking how do I—we—save her?"

Suddenly, Iole sat straight up.

"And *I'm* thinking," Iole cried, "that we should let Pandy take it from here! Hey, Pandy!"

And all eyes turned toward Pandy standing at the entrance. No one moved for a long moment. Then, very slowly, someone began to clap. And someone else joined in. Soon the room was full of the sound of a rhythmic applause; not wild, but measured and enthusiastic.

"Well . . . sure," said Alcie, realizing that she had totally lost her audience. "Now that she's here. Of course. Pandy! Whoo-hoo!"

"Why were they clapping for me?" Pandy asked Iole in a low voice as she approached the table, the applause dying out.

"Because, believe it or not," Iole whispered, "Alcie did a magnificent job of telling everyone how you undertook the quest all alone and how brave you've been. She recounted the whole story of the box and Zeus and Jealousy just as it happened. Then she started talking about the black whirlwind and the sea and the dolphins and suddenly it became all about her. I think she's got river water on the brain. But that's when you came in."

"Why Cantonese?" Pandy asked.

"You were sleeping when Scylla and Charybdis gave Alcie and me a tour of the camp," Iole answered. "It was a tour of the world. This is kind of a traveling circus and everyone in the troupe comes from someplace completely different. And we understood everyone! But Wang Chun Lo finally explained that most of these people have been with his caravan so long that his native Cantonese is the language almost everybody knows."

"Ah! The last of our little fishes has jumped out of the river of sleep."

Pandora turned and saw the old man standing before her, his hands thrust deep into the opposing sleeves of his deep orange robe, his black braid gathered in many loops at the back of his neck. He regarded her intently for a moment and she felt he was going to say something using only his mind as before.

"No, not tonight." He smiled and opened his mouth to speak, his polished, jagged teeth catching the light of the lamps, his actual voice just as high and gravelly as she'd heard it in her head. "That tool is only used when I am suspicious and wish to probe the recesses of someone's mind. For example, four young companions walking out of a cursed burial tomb. That's a cause for suspicion, don't you think? Now that I know who you are, it is unnecessary. However, that ability pales compared with what your friend says *you* are capable of, my dear Pandora."

"Oh, well . . . Alcie probably just meant . . . ," Pandy began.

A candied orange rind flew out of nowhere and hit the old man on his wrinkled cheek.

He did not turn around, but merely closed his eyes and sighed softly.

"Pandora," he began, extending his left hand out toward the old woman, who was dressed in bright red and glaring from her perch on a high yellow pillow. "Allow me to present my most honored mother, Mai Fung Tan, second dynasty, ruler of the Hunan provinces, consort to Ang Li Fat—He Who Was Truth Bringer, Fire Breather, and Collector of Ladies' Fans—first wife to Lee Hung Lee, third dynasty, He of the Small Ears, and fourth wife to Chan Kwong Lo, eighth dynasty, He Who Sleeps Much."

"Bow," whispered Iole.

"Bow!" Alcie repeated urgently. "We learned the hard way."

The old woman clutched a handful of orange rinds menacingly. Pandy put on her most solemn face and bowed very low to the old woman, who remained motionless except for her twitching fingers.

"She is also an excellent fortune-teller and our

biggest money maker," the old man whispered. "I am Wang Chun Lo. You are most welcome. I trust you slept well?"

"Yes, thank you," Pandy said.

"Splendid. And now, as your companions have done, you will eat and refresh yourself further and then perhaps you will finish your tale."

He beckoned her toward a large, fluffy apricot-colored cushion. The subtlest flick of his forefinger called to a host of servants hovering nearby and seconds later the table was crowded with silver bowls, each holding something delectable. Large prawns and blackened walnuts glazed with honey. Asparagus tips and flat brown mushroom heads, steamed with a sauce that was slightly bitter but delicious—what she imagined salted cream would taste like. A whole fish was encrusted with a coarse seasoned salt that made the taste zing all over her tongue. Little light brown rolls, like tiny pillows—crunchy on the outside, yet warm and soft inside—were filled with many vegetables, some familiar, others unknown. Certain flavors were light and delicate, others very rich. Some dishes had odd textures, and others had one scent but a completely different taste. To drink, there was hot, sweet jasmine tea.

"Oh, I'm so sorry," Wang Chun Lo said, observing Pandy silently devouring everything. "Since you make no sound, I assume that you are only eating to be polite."

Pandy looked up, not realizing that she might be being rude.

"I don't understand," she said.

"It is customary in China to show pleasure with one's food. Perhaps you do not like it? Shall I take it away and . . ."

"No!" Pandy said, throwing her arms out over the table. "I mean no, thank you . . . this is delicious. This is wonderful!"

"Then I am glad. I apologize that these are only the second-best dishes of my country," Wang Chun Lo said. "My cook refuses to repeat himself from one night to the next, and as we expected you last night, naturally he prepared his specialties for you then. Water beetles in oyster sauce, caterpillars in dry mustard, shark fin and quail egg porridge. Ah, well . . . perhaps you shall have another opportunity to taste them."

"Yum!" said Alcie. "What a shame we missed all that!"

Pandy sent a mental thank-you to Morpheus for having knocked her out so completely for an entire day. Then she pinched Alcie.

"Ow! Okay, I'll be good."

When Pandy had emptied all the bowls (with a great deal of loud chewing), a feat at which even the old woman, Mai Fung Tan, had just stared, she sank into the apricot pillow and gave an unexpected but tremendous burp. Wang Chun Lo clapped his hands in delight, then again raised his forefinger and the entire tent fell silent, waiting.

"Pandora," he began. "I believe we had just come to the part where your companion, Alcie, had caught you in her arms as the whirling black wind threw you from the ship, shielding you from harm as you splashed into the ocean. No . . . wait . . . we were past that. Ah, yes, what happened after Alcie led the dolphins to your rescue? No . . . no . . . wait . . . we were past that as well. What happened after Alcie spotted the place for your landing in Egypt?"

Pandy slowly turned to look at Alcie.

Alcie cleared her throat and smiled coyly.

"Well . . . ," Pandy began.

She told of the Chamber of Despair, from first falling though the desert floor to at last reemerging onto the temple terrace. When she finished, the tent was silent again. Then a huge man with a red braid who called himself Olaf held aloft a double-headed ax in salute and called out a greeting in Vik, the ancient language of the Vikings. Pandy smiled and answered back. One by one, members of the troupe rose and introduced themselves. Usumacinta hailed her in lyrical Mayan. Four beautiful, black-haired Arabian girls—Almase, Mahfouza, Nabile, and Sabahat—sang out in unison while a bald woman, Mehlika, wearing a turquoise top and yellow pants, said hello in a biting Hittite dialect. Two girls the color of rust stood up and spoke in rapid Ethiopian. Pandy gasped to see that they were actually joined together at the waist and had only three legs between them. Then three tiny men with red dots on their foreheads greeted her in Hindi as others called out hellos. Latin. Gallic. Persian. Anatolian.

Pandy, Alcie, Iole, and Homer answered them all.

"Even knowing how you came by this knowledge of languages makes it no less amazing to witness," said Wang Chun Lo. He turned to the crowd. "And now that we have all dined well and truly met our guests, it is time . . ."

The crowd groaned.

"No! Not yet! Let's hear more!" came resounding cries.

Wang Chun Lo calmly withdrew his gnarled hands from within his orange robe. "Need I remind you that not only was your practice interrupted yesterday due to the unexpected arrival of our most honored guests, but that our last show in Peking was—how shall I put it?—abysmal."

"But we're a joke! People expect us to be abysmal," said Olaf.

"We're always terrible," said Usumacinta, over a murmur of general agreement.

"We're not!" Wang Chun Lo shot back, a brittle sharpness in his voice. At once, everyone was silent. "We do not travel the world, erecting these pavilions and taking men's coin only to be thought of as disappointing! Perhaps we have slight miscalculations here and there, but I do not pay you to be second rate! We are not jokes! We are performers, my friends, not merely oddities for casual viewing."

Pandy looked at the two Ethiopian girls, sitting in a bizarre three-cross-legged position.

"Each one of you is a walking miracle, and together we are a collection of—"

"Whimsical Manifestations of Nature's Good Humor," they all said in unison.

"Yes! And if your manifestations are to be ready for the city of Alexandria and the young queen Cleopatra, your skills must be much, much sharper. Which reminds me, everyone, brush up on your Egyptian."

"I don't need any practice," croaked Mai Fung Tan. "I am as sharp as a knife. You dishonor your mother and your ancestors to say that my skills of sight and prophecy are otherwise."

With that, she leaned far forward off her yellow cushion and grabbed Homer's right hand, stretching it out across the small table. Homer, who didn't even twitch when he'd have a finger or toe sewn back on by the school physician after every sparring match at gladiator school, now froze in terror at the old woman's touch; unblinking, she held his palm to her yellowed eyes, dragging a long nail across his skin.

Wang Chun Lo sighed to himself.

"The soul of a scribe," Mai Fung Tan began, searching the lines in Homer's hand. "Ah . . . there is a great legacy. Wondrous! Oh, there has been much pain. You turned your back on your father's wishes. Your father does not approve or understand your choices. Ah, but your mother would have, had she lived."

Homer's face went slack.

"You have a great love of words and a glorious future. All will know your name. As your ancestors before, you will write things that will transcend space and generations. I see something else . . . something, no . . . some-one new to you has touched your heart in a strange way. Unexpected. A young—"

Homer snatched his hand away, startling the old woman.

"I . . . I . . . think I'll go check on Dido," he said, standing. "He's probably hungry. Or . . . something." He left the tent, throwing the flap back so hard that it caught on itself and remained open, showing the moonlit desert illuminated beyond.

Mai Fung Tan watched Homer leave, her eyes narrowing into slits. Then she smiled, showing teeth even more sharply pointed than her son's.

She looked smugly at Wang Chun Lo. "I don't need any practice!"

"Honored mother," said Wang Chun Lo, with a slight

roll of his eyes. "You are correct as usual. But your wonders are simpler, a private matter outside the main pavilion, between you and your customers. I speak only of the others. Forgive me."

He gazed out at the crowd, silent for a few moments, as a smile slowly creased the corners of his mouth.

"With new guests and new stories come new thoughts and new ideas," he said at length. "Friends," his voice rising slightly, "we have a fresh audience right here in our midst. Let us practice tonight with an actual show! Costumes, wizardry, lights, and magic! Spare nothing! You have only moments to prepare—be off!"

CHAPTER TWENTY-ONE

Wang Chun Lo's Caravan of Wonders

8:43 p.m.

The entire troupe cleared the tent in a frenzy of colors, shouts, clangs, cheers, and clashes. The next minute, the tangerine tent was almost empty except for Pandy, Alcie, Iole, and Wang Chun Lo. His mother had disappeared, seemingly in a puff of smoke. Servants began pushing tables, cushions, and rugs back against the fabric walls, clearing a large empty circle in the center.

"What's happening? Where did everyone go?" Pandy asked, her curiosity bubbling.

Wang Chun Lo looked at the servants, who nodded in unison, then they too disappeared as Wang Chun Lo walked slowly toward the center of the tangerine tent. Several more oil lamps had been lit but the light didn't shine out in all directions. Instead, their beams focused on a specific area of the tent. A few shone their light directly into the center, making that area almost as bright as day.

Wang Chun Lo spread his arms wide as he glided noiselessly, his orange robe blending with the tangerine, melon, and apricot cushions and the fabric walls until he appeared to be nothing more than a long, black braided queue floating through space. Reaching the center, he turned back toward Homer and the girls. Suddenly, they could focus only on his eyes, reflecting the strong beams of red light from the lamps. With a jangle of the coin ribbons in his hands, he began to speak, his voice and manner now those of a great storyteller.

"Honored guests, elders, and young ones. Highborn and slave. All are welcome, and tonight all are one. For tonight, there are no boundaries between thought and action, light and shadow, real and unreal. Tonight, you shall each share the experience of delight and amazement.

"My friends, there are places in this world where the sun refuses to shine, strange rituals are commonplace, up is down, and in is out. We shall take you there, the places not shown on any map . . . rarely seen by human eyes. For the next few moments we shall remove you from the dreary day-to-day existence of your modern lives with its ease and comforts . . ."

Pandy, Alcie, and Iole looked sideways at each other.

". . . and you shall see a woman fly, grown men no

larger than newborn babes, and a man of the north so fierce he destroyed his country's foes with a single blow. All this I promise you—and more! You will be shocked! Amazed! But remember: there is absolutely nothing to fear. Prepare yourself, my friends, for it all begins . . . *now!*"

He shook his coin ribbons violently. Then, with a clap of his hands, the oil lamps went out and the tent was plunged into complete darkness.

"Apples," whispered Alcie.

"Why am I suddenly frightened?" asked Iole.

"I think it's wonderful," said Pandy. She struggled to remain alert, looking for any clues as to something that might help her; but she knew she was quickly falling under the spell of the caravan.

Two oil lamps seemed to flicker on by themselves, their beams illuminating the center of the tent where Usumacinta now stood dressed in one of her feathered robes. Singing beautifully and turning slowly in a circle, her song told the story of a Mayan princess, a girl born so lovely that the Feathered Serpent Quetzalcoatl, Mayan God of the Morning Star, fell in love with her and sent parrots and hummingbirds to fetch her to him. After each sentence, Usumacinta would pause and one of her bright green birds would fly down through an opening at the top of the tent, landing at her feet. Soon there were ten birds at her feet, each one taking its place in one of two small pyramids: three birds on the bottom, two on top. As Usumacinta finished, a hundred hummingbirds flew into the tent, alighting on her arms and in her hair. Singing the last notes, telling how the princess was saddened to leave her village but joyous about her new life with Quetzalcoatl, Usumacinta stepped lightly onto the two parrot pyramids and all the birds together lifted her off the ground and into the air. She held the final note, clear as the ringing of a wind chime, as she flew through the opening and out into the night.

Pandy, Alcie, and Iole were stunned.

"I think that is the most beautiful thing I've ever seen," said Pandy finally.

"Hades didn't send birds when he wanted Persephone to be his wife. He just pulled her onto his black chariot while she was walking in a field one day," said Alcie.

"No imagination," said Iole.

They began clapping wildly.

From out of the darkness came the voice of Wang Chun Lo.

"Now we take you east to India. To the land of Buddha, Vishnu, and Kali. To the land of Krishna, Shakti, and Brahma. To the land of . . ."

Suddenly, outside the tent there was a sharp yell, a loud squawk, a dull thud, and a moan.

". . . to the land of . . ."

"They dropped me . . . again!" Usumacinta's voice rose outside.

"We keep telling you, you're eating too much!" came another voice.

"I am not, you dried-up lizard," Usumacinta said.

". . . *to the land of* . . . ," Wang Chun Lo continued.

"If they drop me once more during a real show, we're all eating parrot for dinner!" Usumacinta yelled.

"Quiet!" Wang Chun Lo cried in a hoarse whisper. "You have finished! Let the others perform."

Pandy, Alcie, and Iole heard a great rustling of feathers and a loud *harrumph*ing sound as Usumacinta herded her birds back to her tent.

"Um . . . ," Wang Chun Lo went on. "Oh yes—to the land of many-armed Shiva, the destroyer, and Ganesha, he of the elephant head. Come with us to India!"

Into the pool of light tumbled the three tiny men. Swiftly, to the odd sounds of unseen instruments, they writhed, jiggled, and bent their bodies into the shapes of the Indian elephant god, Ganesha, then into the form of Buddha, with his legendary helmet of snails, or Hanuman, the monkey god, and other exotic Indian deities. Sometimes they simply twisted themselves into knots and then, in a flash, they unraveled. At the very end of their act, as the lamps in front of them were extinguished, they stood one upon the other in silhouette and portrayed the goddess Shiva, the destroyer of the world in Indian culture, with her four arms. Just as they were wiggling their arms up and down to represent Shiva's ferocity, one arm hit another arm, which hit another arm, which hit someone's head, which sent the trio collapsing to the floor in a way that left everyone who was watching in hysterics. In silhouette, the three men tried to stand again, and again only to trip over a leg here or an arm there. Finally they began pummeling each other, cursing in small high voices until the dark outlines of three servants grabbed hold of each of the Hindi men and carted them, like infants, out of the tent.

And so it went. Every act, every performance began beautifully and ended with something going wrong in such a way that caused Pandy, Alcie, and Iole to laugh so hard they began to hurt with each breath.

Mehlika, the Hittite woman wearing the turquoise top and yellow pants, entered the tent, this time also wearing a full black wig. She was a human torch who could throw flames with her breath; but more than that, she painted whole pictures in the air with nothing but fire. For several minutes she created seascapes complete with ships, animals grazing in pastures, chariot races, trees in the wind. Then she tried to paint women dancing in a circle and inadvertently lit her head on fire. Two servants standing in the shadows were obviously prepared and immediately doused her with water from wooden buckets. Screeching, she dashed outside and Pandy heard her grumbling to someone nearby that she was running out of horsetail hair for her wigs.

Olaf, the Viking, the "fierce man of the north," rode in standing on the backs of two oversized horses waving his double-headed ax—which flew off its shaft halfway through his act of ax-throwing marksmanship and, narrowly missing a terrified servant, split one of the smaller tent poles in two.

The Ethiopian sisters, joined at the hip, brought forth ferocious, brightly colored cats on long chains. With one sister singing a haunting African melody and the other accompanying on a crude clay flute, the animals were supposedly kept from attacking either their trainers or the unsuspecting audience. The act went well, with the sisters moving gracefully around the center of the tent, until the cats got bored, curled up, and went to sleep.

Then a cage was lowered into the tent through the hole at the top. Inside a man was battling the red snake Pandy had seen in the makeshift corral. As the cage hit the floor, its door flew open and the man and snake burst from inside to begin dueling in the ring of light. Sometimes rising to a height of almost two meters, the snake slinked and slithered as it pretended to bite in what was, to all appearances, a deadly battle. Finally, after subduing the snake, the man coaxed it to coil itself around his body; he was completely encased within seconds, and proceeded to roll around the tent, with the snake, in a wide circle. When it came time for the snake to release him, however, the snake only coiled tighter and the man had to be carried from the tent, his face turning purple, with several servants trying to pull the serpent off him.

"Do you notice how the servants know exactly what to do?" asked Iole.

"They're the real stars of the show," said Pandy.

Alcie said nothing. Only a moment earlier she had felt a slight shift on a cushion close by and realized that Homer had slipped back into the tent and was watching the show.

They saw the "strange" two-eyed Cyclops, the giant dwarf, and the thousand-year-old man with the face of boy.

"Figs! Those are just plain men," whispered Alcie, in the dark.

"You are an unbelie-e-e-ever," giggled Iole.

Pandy wondered for an instant if any of them were the key for which she should be hunting.

There were Balinese shadow puppets, one of which lost its head in the middle of the act. Scylla and Charybdis did a routine full of bad jokes in Greek. The strange animals, the goats with long horns, and the half-horse, half-dog beasts were brought in, to the special delight of Iole.

Suddenly, all of the oil lamps were relit and the four beautiful Arabian girls entered the tent with a *swoosh* of brightly colored silk scarves and a light tinkling of metal. The black-garbed servants shed their dark covering to reveal gold pantaloons and silver vests. They sat and took up stringed instruments, drums, and flutes. One of the girls shook a small, flat drum with metal discs high over her head. The others had these same metal discs attached to their fingers. They struck a dramatic pose and there was silence in the tent. Pandy, Alcie, and Iole held their breath at the sight, but Alcie managed to notice that Homer had silently slipped out yet again.

In a rush of sound and color, the musicians began to play and the girls to dance. Whirling skirts in green, blue, pink, and red, black hair flying in all directions, fingers clinking, and lovely faces hidden by opaque silks—then revealed again and again as they spun in fast circles. Then there were different movements as the girls undulated in unison like tall reeds, forcing their bellies in and out, shaking their hips, the coins sewn to their garments jingling.

As the music grew faster, the four girls began a series of highly intricate steps then finished with a set of furious whirls, with both musicians and girls stopping with a flourish at precisely the same moment.

"What went wrong?" asked Alcie, as Pandy and Iole beat their hands together.

"Nothing!" cried Pandy. "Not one thing!"

"Okay . . . then, whoo-hoo!" yelled Alcie.

The tent was plunged into blackness once more. The air shifted almost imperceptibly and the small hairs on Pandy's arms stood straight up as she strained to see in the dark.

One by one, the lamps illuminating the center flickered back on. On the floor was the empty cage of carved ivory that Pandy had seen the day before. Seven servants entered carrying five very large rectangular panels of a hard, clear substance and small stands on which the panels were placed to stand upright, forming a semicircle around the cage.

Pandy remembered a set of crystals she'd seen once in a market stall in Athens. These panels looked exactly like those hard stones, the same fine cracks running through them, barely perceptible, only these panels had been cut from crystals that were enormous.

The servants departed and there was silence.

Slowly, the clear crystal began to cloud; a fine, white smoke passing through each panel. Then muted colors began to appear, then general shapes: a hillside, the corner of a building, a tall column. Pictures were drawing themselves inside the crystal and the shapes became more distinct. The hillside now had fruit trees and bushes with a road passing through. The corner of the building had a flowing fountain carved into its side. And the tall column was part of a temple where people walked up and down a series of nearby steps and a man sold incense and oranges from a rickety cart. A scene of a field had cows grazing and a picture of snow-covered flatlands had small, crude homes with lights in their windows.

All at once, Pandy, Alcie, and Iole saw Wang Chun Lo descend the steps of the temple in the crystal. He stopped only for a moment to take a stick of incense from the vendor. Then, looking directly ahead, he walked right up to the panel and passed through into the center of the tent.

"Huh?" said Alcie.

Wang Chun Lo bowed deeply from side to side as if he were in front of a large audience. He held the stick of incense high and with a snap of his fingers, lit it on fire. He placed it in the ivory cage, where it smoked lightly, filling the tent with the aroma of sandalwood.

Then Wang Chun Lo stepped into the panel with the building and its fountain. Taking a piece of cloth from the folds of his robe, he soaked the fabric in the water, then crossed out of view and immediately reappeared in the snow scene. He placed the cloth on the frozen ground, walked around the crude house, then he picked up the piece of cloth, which had now frozen solid.

Again, he walked back through the crystal and into the tent. He tapped the frozen cloth against the ivory cage where it made a tinny, clinking sound. With another snap, he lit another fire at his fingertips and held it to the cloth. As the ice melted, the water dripped off the cloth and it became pliable once more. This too Wang Chun Lo put into the ivory cage.

Once more he stepped through a panel, this time onto the hillside with its fruit trees. He swiftly plucked two apples from a tree, took a bite out of one, and left the picture. Suddenly, he was walking up to a bewildered cow in the pasture and holding out the other apple in his hand. The cow took one bite before Wang Chun Lo whisked it away and began to stride toward the panel. As he stepped again into the tent, holding the two apples up high, everyone heard a soft thud as the cow tried to follow Wang Chun Lo, only to bump its nose against the strange barrier. Alcie and Iole began to laugh through their astonishment at the cow's bewilderment, its large pink nose smearing the crystal. Pandy, however, was silent.

As the cow wandered away, Wang Chun Lo placed both apples into the ivory cage. Then he swung the cage slowly from one side of the tent to the other, displaying the contents for all to see.

He closed the small cage door and passed it once behind his back. When he held the cage up again, the contents were gone and there was something new inside. He opened the cage door and withdrew a snow white dove.

"Gods!" said Iole.

Wang Chun Lo held the bird high, then quickly released it into the scene of the hillside, where the bird flew up and landed on a high branch of the nearest apple tree.

Wang Chun Lo turned, waved his hand past the five panels causing them all to go completely clear once more, then bowed very low to his audience.

Alcie and Iole were on their feet, whooping and cheering. Even the servants and a few of the other performers who had snuck in were clapping wildly.

Only Pandy sat stock-still.

Her brain had locked onto one thought as soon as she'd seen the wondrous panels and her mind was racing with possibilities. This had to be the "interesting force" to which Artemis had guided her! Pandy became more and more excited. If this were nothing more than a trick then her idea was out of the question. But if it was as she suspected, that Wang Chun Lo actually had the ability to easily move through different parts of the world, then . . .

Suddenly, Pandy was jolted by Iole's firm tug on her arm.

"Pandy," Iole was saying. "Didn't you like it?"

"What?" she mumbled.

Snapping out of her daydream, she saw much commotion at the center of the tent. The last of the panels was being carried out of the tent as the musicians took to their instruments once again. One by one the performers were entering to take their bows. Pandy began to clap, but she thought only of her plan. She was trying to think of how she could best explain her idea to Wang Chun Lo when the four Arabian dancers entered. Instead of bowing, they began their dance again, everyone joining in the celebration. All except Wang Chun Lo, who was nowhere to be seen.

Even though most of the performers were somewhat worse for wear, the music was lively and the dancing was infectious, and soon everyone was doing his or her own version of a belly dance. Then Almase, Mahfouza, Nabile, and Sabahat danced their way over to Pandy, Alcie, and Iole, beckoning them.

All three froze, and Pandy forgot her plan altogether.

Almase took hold of Iole's hand while Mahfouza led Pandy into the circle. But it required both Nabile and Sabahat to tackle Alcie as she tried to crawl away over the orange cushions.

"I can't dance!" she wailed, unheard in the din. "I can barely walk!"

On the floor, Mahfouza smiled down at Pandy, circling her with a series of quick turns. From far away, these girls seemed to be rare birds, not really girls at all; surely nothing human could move like that. Up close, Pandy saw they were even lovelier than she imagined. A picture of her mother flashed again in her mind. These girls were just as beautiful, perhaps even more so. And then, even though Jealousy was trapped securely in the wooden box in her leather carrying pouch, Pandy remembered what it had felt like when it consumed her so completely in the Temple of Apollo at Delphi. Was she experiencing it again? Jealousy of these girls, whom she could never be like in a million moons? She stood like stone in the center of the tent, too petrified to move no matter how much the music enticed her.

If she didn't move, she thought, she would never know exactly how embarrassed she could be; how her clumsy body might betray her in front of these girls who were . . . perfect. If she stayed still, she could avoid at least some humiliation and try to concentrate on explaining her plan to Wang Chun Lo.

But Mahfouza would have none of it. She stopped whirling and, gently, took Pandy's hands in hers, swaying slowly from side to side. Pandy had almost no choice but to follow. She looked at Iole, who was moving with Almase and smiling broadly, and Alcie, who appeared to be laughing with Nabile and Sabahat, but still remained motionless, her arms folded defiantly across her chest.

Pandy looked back at Mahfouza and, abandoning her own thoughts for a moment, tried to keep up. She felt so foolish. And then, as if she had drunk a strange elixir, the music found its way into her bones. Her head cleared of everything and she thought of nothing but the rhythms around her. Suddenly her feet were moving on their own. Her arms found a new energy and they mirrored Mahfouza's movements exactly. She swayed back and forth, watching Mahfouza's feet, trying each new step, every little variation. Then Mahfouza spun around several times and Pandy's jaw dropped. Mahfouza laughed and did it again. I was only after the third time that Pandy just let herself go. She spun and stopped. Perfect. She spun again and again and again. Then she fell down.

Laughing hard, Mahfouza helped Pandy up, then taught her how to look at a certain point in the tent every time she whirled to keep from getting dizzy. Soon Pandy was spinning almost as fast as the "rare birds" she thought so lovely. Her arms were swaying and she was perfectly in step.

And a new feeling crept into her soul. The tiniest hint of a notion. That on this night she just might be feeling what it's like to be a full-grown woman. Pretty. Attractive. Feminine. No longer awkward in her own skin, but graceful, comfortable, and strong. How her beautiful mother must feel every moment of her life . . .

when she isn't in a jar. She began to really smile, which only made Mahfouza laugh all the more.

Pandy looked at Iole to see if she was feeling the same. Iole's dancing was anything but graceful—her legs and arms seemed to be about a beat behind the music—but it was plain from the look in her eyes that she was having the time of her life.

Then Pandy turned to find Alcie.

Because of her two left feet, Alcie couldn't manage the basic steps no matter how hard she tried. However, in the few moments they had been learning to dance, she had become a master spinner—to the right. Nabile and Sabahat were dancing again themselves, Iole was enjoying herself too much, as was everyone else, so it was only Pandy who watched Alcie, giggling wildly, spin herself through a loose flap in the tent wall and out into the desert night.

That sight was all the jolt Pandy needed to focus again. She stopped dancing and walked quickly to Iole.

As good a time as she was having, Iole saw the serious look on Pandy's face and instantly stood still.

"What's wrong?"

"Nothing's wrong. Everything's right," Pandy said. "I think I know how we can get to Alexandria . . . tonight!"

CHAPTER TWENTY-TWO

A Conversation

9:57 p.m.

Pandy and Iole ran out of the tangerine tent as the dancing continued inside.

The spot where Alcie had tumbled through was now on the farthest side away from them.

"This way is shorter," said Iole, running to the left.

"No, this way," Pandy answered, dashing off to the right.

"All right. Great Aphrodite, it doesn't really matter," said Iole racing past Pandy.

When they arrived at the place where Alcie should have been, however, she was nowhere to be found; only the bottom of the tent jumbled in upon itself and two left-foot tracks leading off a short distance before disappearing completely.

"Alcie!" Pandy cried. They were on the perimeter of the camp, now completely deserted. Pandy saw the silver slug trail only a few meters away, hoping against hope that Alcie hadn't stumbled into it.

"Come on."

They ran as fast as they could to Usumacinta's garlic-shaped tent. It too was deserted.

"Where did she go?" asked Iole.

"All right," said Pandy. "First, we find Wang Chun Lo. I have to speak to him right now. Then we'll find Alcie. I'm sure she's back in the main tent or she found the cooking tent and she's eating again or . . . or . . . I don't know, but she's around somewhere." The notion that Alcie might have accidentally fried herself like a little beetle sent a shiver up Pandy's spine, but she didn't want to unnecessarily alarm Iole.

Unbeknownst to either of them, Alcie was in none of those places.

Alcie sat up on the sandy ground, having just crashed her way through the tent, and batted at the heavy fabric still caught around her feet. As she cleared the last of it away, she burst into tears.

She stood up and tried to walk in a straight line back toward the garlic-shaped tent but, as usual, her feet kept taking her to the right. She was so tired of her miserable condition (her "bipedal challenge," as Iole called it) that every step brought more tears. She realized that, as she danced, she'd been happy for the first time in days. Every rare, fleeting moment of joy since she'd left Athens was consistently taken from her as soon as it arrived. She gave up struggling against her feet and just veered, willy-nilly, into the camp, weeping dejectedly and not very softly.

Suddenly, she hit a tree. Before she could fall backward, however, two massive arms caught her and stood her upright again.

Alcie looked up in the light from the half moon and saw Homer staring down at her.

"Oh . . . hi," she said, turning her face away.

"Hi."

"I'm sorry I walked into you. I thought you were a tree. Not to say that I walk into trees. I just . . . oh, apples," she said, a quiver in her voice, "wasn't paying much attention."

Homer continued to hold her by her arms. Alcie, even though she was terribly embarrassed that he was seeing her crying and disheveled, let herself just . . . kinda . . . collapse. And still he held her. After a moment, he picked her up and carried her to the circle of animal cages in the center of the camp. He found two that were empty, placed her gently on top of one, and sat down himself on the other, which promptly exploded underneath him.

"I'll stand."

"Thanks. For . . . carrying me . . . for that," said Alcie. Then she began crying again. "I just can't walk anymore!"

Homer was silent for a long time. So long, in fact, that Alcie had time to stop sniffling. She began to think he was just tolerating her; that he really thought she was foolish, with her wisecracking mouth and bizarre feet. Her situation wasn't really her fault in the first place! Okay, so she wasn't Pandy, and she was certain that she'd seen the way he looked at Pandy. Why was he even being nice to her? And then she started to get angry.

"Lemons. I'm gonna go . . ."

"Can I read something to you?" he said abruptly.

"Um. Okay," she answered hesitantly. "What I mean is, of course you can. May. You may. Yes. Please."

"It's a poem."

"Oh! Huh? A what?" she cried, then, "When did you write a poem?"

"Just now. But I've been working on it in my head for a few hours."

Homer unfolded a small piece of parchment.

"What's it about?"

"Just some thoughts," Homer replied, but his hands were shaking slightly.

He cleared his throat twice and began to read, never taking his eyes from the page.

The poem wasn't very long; it contained a few words that Alcie didn't understand exactly, she only knew that hearing them gave her an odd feeling in the pit of her stomach, like she had swallowed butterflies. Then she realized it was a love poem . . . actually more of a "deep, deep like" poem. It was about a boy and a girl who came from different worlds, but he had grown to care about her in the short time they'd known each other.

And then Alcie's stomach dropped out of her body and onto the ground. It was about Pandy. He used words like funny, smart, loyal, lovely, and courageous. At least, Alcie determined, the bigger words he used meant exactly those same things. She felt herself getting ill. Suddenly, it occurred to Alcie that it was far too dark for him to be able to read anything: he'd memorized every word. And now he wanted her opinion; after all, she knew Pandy almost better than anyone in the world. How cruel this was. She hung her head, wanting to be anywhere else. The Chamber of Despair, the flames of Tartarus, anywhere. But something ugly inside made her stay until he finished, as if she wanted to see how bad it could actually get, this new feeling of her heart eating its way out of her chest.

And then it was over.

Neither of them moved.

"I guess you don't like it," Homer said finally, the hand with the parchment dropping slowly to his side.

"Prunes," Alcie said to herself. Then she did the bravest thing, she was certain, she'd ever done. She raised her head and looked right at him.

And she smiled.

"It's just wonderful," she said. "It's better than anything I've ever heard. And . . . and . . ."

She paused, fighting back tears.

". . . I'm sure she'll really, really like . . ."

Then Homer bent way down and kissed her. Very softly. And rather fast. Not quite on her mouth, but close to it; close enough so she understood.

"I'm sorry I did that," he blurted out. "Okay . . . um . . . not really. But I just don't know if I'll get another chance . . . to tell you. You're very cool. Uh . . . special. At least, I think so. Anyway, I hoped you'd like the poem."

"Huh?"

Homer only smiled.

As her heart thumped wildly, perfectly at home in her chest, Alcie thought of all the great moments in her life. The first time she laced her sandals by herself. The instant when she knew she and Pandy had become best friends. The day she heard four other girls in the Athens marketplace say that she had the prettiest eyes of anyone they knew. The moment she decided to help Pandy on her quest.

This moment topped them all.

CHAPTER TWENTY-THREE

The Private Tent

10:08 p.m.

"Alcie!"

Iole and Pandy came running up to Alcie and Homer as a few of the performers began to filter back through the camp.

"Oh good, Homer, you're here too. Alcie, we've been looking all over—Gods!" Pandy interrupted herself. "Alcie . . . are you all right? You've been crying."

"Are you hurt?" asked Iole.

Alcie smiled.

"Not a bit," she said. Hopping down from the cage, she stumbled back slightly only to be caught again by Homer.

"Never been better," she said with utmost sincerity. "What's up?"

"We have to find Wang Chun Lo," said Pandy.

"Pandy has an idea," said Iole. "Although I still don't think he'll let us do it."

"Do what?" asked Alcie.

"Come on," said Pandy, heading off toward the other side of the camp.

"Wait," said Alcie. "If you want to find him, why don't we just go back to the big orange?"

"Tangerine," said Iole.

"Tangerine, orange! Figs, let's just go back there."

"Because," said Pandy, marching on, "that's the show tent and the feast tent. It's sort of the general, all-purpose tent, I think. He's got to have private quarters and I'm going to find them."

"Well . . . all right then," said Alcie, struggling to hurry. Without warning, Homer was at her right side, his hand almost imperceptibly on her elbow, guiding her straight ahead.

They poked their heads into the pistachio, jar, and floor-pillow tents. All of them were still empty and there was no clue that any of these might be the private tent of Wang Chun Lo.

Pandy was about to look into the sky-colored staircase tent when she caught the shiny gray mass of the slow-moving slug tent out of the corner of her eye. She dashed off in its direction.

"Excuse me?" she said, calling up to the sentry at the head. "Excuse me, Shahriyar, is it? Hello?" Without even looking down, he pointed toward the rear of the slug, indicating that anyone who might speak to her would only be back there.

She walked swiftly to the rear as Iole, Alcie, and Homer caught up.

"What is this?" asked Alcie.

"We didn't see this when we got our tour," said Iole.

"It's the sentry tent," said Pandy. "Whatever you do, don't walk in the slime trail."

"And you needed to warn me *not* to do that . . . why?" asked Alcie.

"It's the main protection for the camp," said Pandy. "It will kill you instantly. Somehow, these men create it."

"Who are they?" asked Iole, looking up at the sentries.

"We are the Caliphs! 'Channels of Earthly Displeasure,'" cried Abdul-Rashid al Ahmed, glaring at Pandy. "Why have you returned, woman?"

"I need your help," said Pandy. "Can you tell me which tent belongs to Wang Chun Lo?"

"I will tell you nothing," snipped Abdul-Rashid. "Already because of you I must shave my head. And now you have brought other women with you? Wait."

He brandished his curved sword at Homer.

"You there, are you a woman?"

"No," said Homer.

"Then I shall speak only to you."

"You have *got* to be kidding," said Alcie loudly.

"Shh!" Pandy whispered. "We don't have time to argue. Homer, will you ask him, please?"

"Uh, can you tell me . . ."

"I'm certain had he wanted you to know, he would have told you himself," Abdul-Rashid interrupted, picking his teeth with tip of his blade.

"Tell him it's very important," whispered Pandy. "A matter of life and death!"

Homer paused.

"Noble sir," he said. "It's really . . . uh . . . not important at all. I just wanted to ask his advice on which of these . . . um . . . women would make the best serving girl. But you're probably right. And when I see him tomorrow, I'll tell him that you . . . y'know . . . thought the question wasn't worth his time. I'll tell him you made the decision for him. So, which one do you think should . . . uh . . . serve me?"

"Brilliant," mused Iole.

Abdul-Rashid was silent so long that they all had to take several steps sideways to keep up with the slug.

"The clearing," he said finally.

"The clearing, oh honorable one?" asked Homer.

"Yes, of course. You see the tents arranged in a circle. Find the longest space between two tents. There you will find Wang Chun Lo."

"Thank you, sir," said Homer, bowing deeply before turning his back on the slug tent.

"I hate him," hissed Alcie, walking away.

"I think you should take the little one," called

Abdul-Rashid from a distance. "The one who doesn't speak much."

"That does it!" said Iole, whirling around.

Homer caught her with his right hand while still piloting Alcie with his left; forcefully guiding both of them back toward the center of the camp.

"There!" said Pandy, surveying the circle and noticing a wide gap between two tents.

"There's nothing here," said Alcie, all four stepping cautiously into the empty clearing. "Unless Wang Chun Lo sleeps on the sand under the stars each night."

"There's nobody even walking in this area," Pandy said. "And it's the shortest route from the main tent to the rest of the camp."

At that moment, she toppled face forward onto the ground—and her head completely disappeared.

"Gods!" said Iole, moving forward. "Pandy!"

"I'm fine," she said, her head reappearing as she sat up, "but there's something here."

"Where?" asked Iole.

"Right here, right in front of me."

"She's right," said Iole holding out her hands. "It's . . . it's some sort of fabric. It's a tent."

"Something else that's invisible that we have to get around," scoffed Alcie.

"Or get into," Pandy replied, grabbing hold of

something unseen with her right hand and sticking her left arm through where it vanished. "How about right here?"

She peeled back an invisible fabric flap, revealing the interior of a brilliantly lit pavilion.

Huge red Chinese lanterns hung down from the top of the tent, which was massive in its size. As Pandy peered deep into the recesses, beyond the carved black lacquer chairs and the paper screens, her eye immediately caught sight of the five clear panels, resting on their stands off to one side.

"Excuse me?" she called out. "May I speak to you, please?"

As the four of them entered the tent, Pandy walked slowly to the panels, examining them carefully. As she went behind each, she asked, "Can you see me?"

"Yes," said Iole.

"Now?"

"Yes," Homer answered.

"Pandy, what are you thinking?" asked Alcie.

"Do not tell them, little fish." Wang Chun Lo was standing directly in front of her, hidden from the others behind a large red lacquered cabinet, communicating with his thoughts. "We shall discuss this privately."

At his motion to follow, Pandy held her hand up as a sign for the others to remain behind.

She followed Wang Chun Lo through a maze of oddly carved furniture, hanging tapestries, cages of small monkeys, and the snow white birds she had seen in his act. He led her to a quiet area with a low table and chairs.

"I have been expecting you," he said silently. "I have followed your thoughts all over my camp tonight; my apologies for the rudeness of my sentry. I must say, you are an extremely resourceful girl with tremendous abilities. Were it not for your pursuit to rid the world of its evils, I should be happy to find a place for you in my caravan. Tea?"

"No thank you, sir," she thought. "There isn't much time . . ."

"I hope you shall discover, as you journey through life, that there is always time . . . for tea."

He passed his hand over the table and a tiny black teapot instantly appeared along with two of the smallest cups she'd ever seen.

"Thank you."

"And, if I can truly help you as you wish, then there is no hurry, is there? You could be wherever you'd like in an instant, yes?"

She saw the hint of a smile at the corners of his mouth.

"The panels," she began, "they're crystal?"

"Ancient crystal, yes."

"Can you help me get to Alexandria through the crystals?"

"Of course. But that is not the question."

Pandy paused.

"Will you help me?"

"Of course. Your quest is righteous and your heart is brave. It would be my honor to assist in whatever small way I can. But that is not the question."

Pandy stared down at her tea.

"The question is not one you must ask of me, little fish, but of yourself. It is simply this: will I be willing to pay the price?"

"Price?"

"Of course. The use of the crystals for transportation forms a break with both time and space. It is against every known law and is, therefore, extremely powerful magic. The gods would not bestow this magic to anyone wishing to use it, even for a good cause, without expecting tribute."

"What is the tribute?" she asked.

Wang Chun Lo quieted his mind for a moment.

"Your youth," he said finally, the smile still hanging at the corners of his mouth.

"My what?"

"Lower your mind's voice, Pandora, I am right here."

Wang Chun Lo took a deep breath.

"Let me be more specific. It is the luster and glow of your skin, the proper functioning of your organs, the strength of your bones. The gods demand your most vital years. Look at me, Pandora. Look closely at my face, my hands, and my neck. In actual age I am not that old, and my mind is still that of a young man, yet my skin tells a different story. Each passage through the crystals takes fifteen cycles of twelve moons each off my entire being. Now my body is so old that any passage creates almost no visible difference."

Pandy wondered what kept Wang Chun Lo alive.

"Very good question, little fish," he replied. "And although you didn't actually inquire, I shall tell you. Tea."

"Tea?"

"This tea. A special restorative blend made by sorcerers in the deepest heart of China. But now you see why there must always be time . . . for tea."

Pandy drank her tea thoughtfully.

"Now, for myself, I have accepted this price willingly to satisfy my desire to see the world. And, of course, the crystals are a source of amazement to our audiences and a rather lucrative stream of income. But will you pay the price? And, more important, will your friends?"

Pandy was thunderstruck. What would she look like fifteen years older? She would still be thirteen, but she'd have the body and face of a twenty-eight-year-old woman. She had wanted to be older; she'd thought

about no longer looking pudgy or getting small blem-
ishes. But she always thought it would happen in the
normal way. Gods, she thought, if the girls back at
school thought she was weird before . . .

"Of course you may travel with us to Alexandria. The
caravan moves slowly, but we will be there in slightly
less than two weeks. Perhaps you could wait?"

"No," Pandy said, not knowing what else Hera might
have in store in the coming two weeks. "I'll do it . . .
alone."

"You will not need your friends, then?"

Of course she needed them. She wouldn't know
what to do or where to go without them. She needed
Iole's brain and Alcie's courage and loyalty. She even
needed Homer. But she couldn't ask them to give up fifteen years of their lives.

Wang Chun Lo touched the fingers of his hands
together delicately.

"I may be able to make you an offer on behalf of the
gods."

Pandy looked at him.

"If you would be willing to accept all of their years
onto yourself, I may be able to keep them as they are
now. But you would all have to pass through at once."

Pandy's jaw dropped. Four times fifteen! She'd take
on sixty years—plus her thirteen.

She was going to be seventy-three years old.

Her mind was reeling. Only an hour before, she had first felt comfortable and feminine in her own skin as she danced with Mahfouza. Now, in order to get where she needed to be, she would have to bypass that potentially beautiful part of herself and become an old woman.

She tilted her head back. What about Dido? She turned to look àt Wang Chun Lo.

"The gods are not interested in your dog, little fish. Dido will remain as he is."

"That's one small consolation," she thought. Her mind wandered for several minutes more. She had once thought the biggest decision she would ever have to make was to try to save the world. Wrong. This one was right up there.

"Oh well," she finally thought, resigned. "I'll probably end up dead before the quest is done anyway."

"Now, now—where is that indomitable spirit?"

"I won't tell my friends what's going to happen," she replied, dodging his question.

"As you wish, Pandora," he said. "Now, exactly where in Alexandria do you want to go?"

"I . . . I . . . don't know."

"Well then," Wang Chun Lo thought. "Your use of the crystals might be futile, don't you think? If you don't know the precise location, you may waste all the precious time you'll be saving. I shall assume that you have never been there before and therefore you know no one."

"That's not true," said Pandy, out loud. "Well, it's true but . . . but I know *of* someone there. I'll be right back."

She wound her way back through the maze of furniture, past her startled friends, and dashed out of the tent, throwing the tent flap back on itself, causing the opening to remain visible.

"Pandy!" cried Iole.

"No time. Be right back. Keep the flap open!"

Sprinting through the camp, she burst into the garlic-shaped tent in seconds, startling Usumacinta, who was putting a foul-smelling ointment on a huge purple bruise just above her knee.

"Hello," said Pandy. "Excuse me."

Rifling through her leather carrying pouch, she found the note given to her by Ankhele, the acolyte at the Temple of the Apollo in Delphi, which directed Pandy to seek any assistance in Alexandria from Ankhele's father, the city tax collector. Clutching it tightly, she thrust her pouch back under the pallet, then thought better of it and hauled out all the girls' belongings. Checking to be sure that she had everything, she loaded herself down and clucked at Dido.

"Thank you very much for the use of your tent," she said to Usumacinta, who had been watching in silent surprise. "Your act is really beautiful. Good luck in Athens when you arrive there, it's a wonderful city. Thanks again. Bye!"

She and Dido rushed out and crossed the camp, stumbling a little from the weight and swing of the pouches.

Ahead she saw the light from the open flap of the invisible tent surrounded by the black desert beyond.

Inside, she quickly dropped the bags and skins on the ground. "Check and see if I got everything. If I didn't, then go back and get it, but you've got to be fast. Really fast. I'll be right back."

Disappearing into the furniture maze before anyone had a chance to speak, she reached Wang Chun Lo, still seated at the low table. She held out Ankhele's note.

"This is the only person I kinda don't really know in Alexandria."

Wang Chun Lo studied the note carefully. Then he closed his eyes and seemed to drift off to sleep. He was so still for so long that Pandy thought the sun would come up again before she would be able to cross into the crystal.

"Come," he said, all at once opening his eyes. He stood and walked back toward the crystal panels. Alcie and Iole had just finished checking their belongings.

"Where's Homer?" asked Pandy.

"He left a few things by the side of Usumacinta's tent," said Iole. "He'll be right back." As she finished, Homer stepped inside. Pandy put her finger to her lips.

Wang Chun Lo stepped to the center panel and waved his hand across the surface. Instantly the crystal grew cloudy, then a city scene, at a great height, slowly appeared. Unlike the scenes in the main tent, however, this picture moved, as if it all were being seen through the eyes of a great bird soaring over Alexandria, the lighthouse flashing in the far distance. Wang Chun Lo waved his hand over Ankhele's note, said something low under his breath and tossed it into the crystal. The note floated on the wind on the other side, bouncing on the air currents, but all the while descending. Lower and lower it fell, over rooftops and darkened streets, until it landed on the doorstep of a large home in the center of the city. A gust of wind scuttled the note through the open door and into the main room, where it finally came to rest at the feet of a distinguished-looking man. The man picked the note off the floor, read it, and began to look rapidly about the room, a look of utter confusion on his face. At this point, Wang Chun Lo himself stepped through the crystal. The startled man had no weapons about him, not expecting an ancient Chinese man to suddenly appear in his home, so he quickly gathered his wife and two small sons behind him and puffed out his chest defiantly.

Wang Chun Lo began to speak, too softly for Pandy to hear, and after some time and with a little hesitation the man relaxed his stance, truly listening to Wang Chun Lo. Every so often the man would look at Pandy through the crystal. She could tell when Wang Chun Lo hit a delicate point or told of something especially incredible, by the man's expressions of shock or relief. She was alternately wondering what exactly Wang Chun Lo was saying and being grateful that she didn't have to explain it herself. Finally, the man walked carefully to the panel gateway. Peering into it, he looked back once over his shoulder, nodding in agreement to something. Wang Chun Lo walked past the man and stepped back into his tent.

"This is the man you seek, little fish," he said to Pandy. "This is Ankhele's father, Asaad. He can hear you through the crystal and he is willing to answer any questions."

Alcie, Iole, and Homer, not knowing that any of this had been brewing in Pandy's brain, were simply struck mute.

"Good evening, sir," said Pandy, putting her best effort into a formal tone of voice and speech.

"Good evening . . . Pandora," Asaad said, staring at her through the crystal. "You bring greetings from my daughter?"

"Yes, sir, I do. Your daughter is well. She is one of the . . . best . . . acolytes in the Temple of Apollo at Delphi. She sends her love to your whole family and she misses you a lot. I mean, a great deal."

"I thank you for that. When we last heard from Ankhele, there was much trouble at the oracle. Something to do with the high priestess."

"I tell you, this is why she should have never left home!" Ankhele's mother spoke up. "Our gods are not exciting enough! Our daughter wants to 'see the world' . . ."

"Kesi! Hush!" cried Asaad.

"That trouble is all over now, sir," said Pandy.

"So I am told," Asaad said. "I am also told that you are responsible for resolving the difficulties."

"Thank you, but we all did it," she said, gesturing to her friends. "Sir, Ankhele said that you might . . . that you would be able to help me."

"I have just been informed of your quest. You seek Vanity in its purest form, is this correct?"

"Yes, sir," she replied. "The map I carry says that Vanity is somewhere here—I mean there—in Alexandria. Do you have any idea where?"

"This is what I know, Pandora," Asaad said, his voice growing grave. "Several weeks ago, reports began to leak out from the royal palace here. As I am in a position of some responsibility, I have access to much information unknown to the average citizen. A strange illness had overcome our young queen, Cleopatra. She would not eat. Physicians were summoned and sacrifices made, but nothing has helped. She has continued to starve herself."

"I'm sorry, sir," said Pandy, interrupting, "but that sounds like she wants to die. I don't know how that can help—"

"You must let me finish," Asaad said. "She has also refused to sleep, or study, or walk among the people she rules. Instead, she does one thing and one thing only: gazes all day and all night, at herself, in her mirror."

"Gods," said Iole, coming up to stand alongside Pandy.

"Only her handmaidens and servants are allowed to approach. They brush her hair constantly; they apply rouge to her cheeks and the blackest kohl around her eyes. They adorn her with the costliest jewels and fabrics. According to some, she has become nothing more than a walking skeleton . . ."

Pandy's mind flashed on the living corpse of Habib.

". . . but she has the strength of twenty men. If anyone dares to paint her lips incorrectly or pin her cloak at the wrong angle, or worse, if they forget to tell her she is the most beautiful creature on the earth, she herself kills them instantly. But these tasks are almost impossible to accomplish."

"Why?" asked Alcie, quietly.

"One of her handmaidens made the mistake weeks ago of trying to gaze into the mirror herself. Cleopatra broke her neck instantly. From that moment, she has allowed no one near it, and to ensure that no one else views their own face, she has had all her servants blinded."

Standing next to Pandy, Iole slumped.

"Where is she now?" asked Pandy, the remains of the feast rising in her throat.

"If what I am told is correct," Asaad said, "she has not ever left her royal apartments. Is this information of assistance to you?"

Pandy looked at Wang Chun Lo, who returned her gaze with a small smile.

"Yes. Thank you, sir," said Pandy.

"It has been my privilege," Asaad replied. "Knowing that you have spoken with our beloved Ankhele only recently has made us feel her absence slightly less. For that, I must thank you."

Wang Chun Lo approached the crystal panel.

"We shall trouble you no further. May the remainder of your evening be pleasant."

Asaad nodded his head as, with a wave of Wang Chun Lo's hand, the panel cleared.

"That was brilliant," said Alcie. "Using these . . . things, whatever they are, to find Ankhele's father. Now we won't have to waste time looking for him."

"Or Vanity," said Iole. "It's her mirror."

"Has to be," Alcie agreed.

Wang Chun Lo and Pandy were staring hard at each other.

"Are you ready?" he asked quietly.

"Yes," she replied.

"Truly?"

Knowing full well what he meant, she faltered for a moment. Then she nodded. "Yes."

With that, he bowed very low.

"I honor you, little fish."

She returned the bow respectfully. Then she turned to her friends.

"Do you have everything?"

"It's all here," said Alcie. "Why?"

"What do we do?" Pandy asked Wang Chun Lo.

"Each of you will take a panel. When I give the signal, you will all step through."

"What?" said Iole.

"Cool," said Homer.

"No," said Alcie.

"Alcie, it's the quickest way there. Period," said Pandy.

"Just because he can do it"—she gestured wildly to Wang Chun Lo, her voice squeaking—"doesn't mean we can. It's magic. It's a trick of some kind. I'll end up with a cow in a field somewhere."

She began to back away.

"No you won't," Pandy said, taking her friend's hand and feeling it tremble. "I promise you, by the wisdom of the Great Athena and the honor of Zeus himself, that nothing will happen to you, except that one moment you'll be here and the next you'll be in Alexandria. Wang Chun Lo has promised and I believe him, Alcie. Plus, we have no time to lose. Alcie, if you have ever trusted me before, please trust me now."

"Unhhh," groaned Alcie, as Pandy led her to a crystal panel.

Homer and Iole slowly took their places as Pandy, grabbing Dido's scruff, stood in front of the center crystal.

"Dido," she said, looking into his face, "you come with me, ghost dog. Understand?"

He barked once.

"Ready," Pandy said to Wang Chun Lo.

Wang Chun Lo waved his hands and the crystals grew cloudy. As the ensuing colors and shapes became more distinct, again each had a bird's-eye view of Alexandria. As the city rose up, the view passed over homes, temples, and odd buildings the likes of which they had not seen in the great metropolis of Athens. Suddenly, an enormous structure emerged before them. The view took them into a dark passageway and down a torch-lit tunnel. Pandy, fleetingly, saw the same drawings she'd seen high in the air in the Chamber of Despair. Then the view took them up and down flights of stairs, down hallways, and through large rooms with many treasures and dozens of strange-looking caskets, only the caskets were empty, their lids thrown off and scattered about the room. Then they were out onto a terrace, down another hallway, into a antechamber, through a set of heavy privacy curtains, and into the royal apartments of Queen Cleopatra.

"Now!" said Wang Chun Lo.

They each stepped through their crystals.

Instantly, they were surrounded by opulence; marble and silk, fountains and gold. Alcie gave a whoop before Iole shushed her. Homer went to Alcie's side. Dido sniffed the air. But Pandy had turned back to look at Wang Chun Lo immediately after crossing over.

He gazed at her from his tent.

"Did it . . . ? Do I . . . ?"

Wang Chun Lo nodded. Then, with a smile and one more low bow, he waved his hand and the panels disappeared.

"That was very interesting," said Iole.

"Apricots, it was nothing!" said Alcie. "Pandy, that was—"

Alcie stopped. Pandy had turned to face them.

"Great Apollo! Pandy!" Alcie screamed.

She looked at her friends now from under cracked and wrinkled lids. Pandy, quite simply, had become an old, old woman.

CHAPTER TWENTY-FOUR

Cleopatra

11:17 p.m.

Every wrinkle, every line was there, just as had been foretold. Her hair was gray and flesh hung loosely from her arms. Although she was still thin, she had several folds of wattling skin under her neck. She looked at her hands: blue veins and mottled skin stretched thinly over each protruding knuckle and all the way up her arms. She felt aches and stiffness in every joint; she was hunched over and couldn't straighten up. She felt her face; there were deep creases along the sides of her mouth and at the corners of her eyes. And she was beginning to realize the horrible actuality of her commitment.

"Pandy?" Alcie asked again.

"Yeah, it's me."

"What happened?" asked Iole, trying hard to be calm and smart and unafraid.

"I don't have time to explain . . . ," she began, realizing that she had almost no teeth.

"Make the time," said Alcie, with unusual authority. "There's no one around. What happened?"

"It's the crystals," she said. "They're enchanted. Every time someone steps through they have fifteen years taken off their . . . life, kinda. That's why Wang Chun Lo looks the way he does. I'm still me. I'm okay inside; it's just my body. It's no big deal."

"It's a very, very big deal," Iole said. "And that's more than fifteen."

"Everyone?" said Alcie, looking at her hands and feeling her face. "Do I look . . . ?"

"No," Pandy said, looking at them through watery eyes. "I made an agreement. I got all of your years, so you guys are fine. We just all had to go through together. And we're here! So, it's good—it's great!"

"You got . . . how many?" Alcie said, calculating. While she was thinking, Iole strode right up to Pandy, eyes blazing.

"You knew and you didn't tell us? I think . . . I think . . . I am so angry with you I don't even have the words. You asked us to trust you and then you do this."

"Iole . . . ?" Pandy said.

"The bottom line is *you* don't trust *us*! To make our own decisions! We should have known about that . . . this. I would have taken my years. I would have been responsible for myself. I didn't come with you, Pandora,

219

so you could baby me. We're . . . we're a team! We're supposed to be. But you treat us like . . . like . . . you're better than us. You keep secrets. And now look at you!"

Iole burst into tears.

Instead of feeling guilty or sorry, instead of trying to understand Iole's point of view, it was Pandy's turn to become very angry.

"Yes!" she screeched. "I did it alone, okay? I didn't tell you! And if I make a decision that's gonna keep you guys from getting even more hurt, then too bad! And I don't care what you think, because I didn't ask you to come with me in the first place. This whole thing is all my fault and I have to think about that every day. If I fail then I'm the one who's going spend the rest of her life in Tartarus, so I get to be the leader—me! Two weeks was way too much to travel. Something could have happened and I need to get these things in the box as fast as possible. So I chose. Me! I'm in charge. Not you. And if you don't like it then you can go home!"

"Whoa," said Homer, quietly.

"Oh, figs," Alcie began. "She didn't mean—"

"Shut up!" Pandy screamed, flecks of spittle flying from her mouth. She stood there, drained and immobile, because the very act of turning her head would have taken too much energy. She was completely at a loss. Even when she tried to do the right thing, some-body, somewhere, somehow was upset.

Iole just stood there with tears streaming down her face.

"Fine," she said, after a moment. "I *will* go home."

"Fine," said Pandy.

"Fine!" Iole yelled.

In that instant, Dido began barking furiously, causing everyone to turn and look.

Five guards, each one larger than Homer, were rapidly advancing. They wore tight-fitting tunics with long gold sashes around the waist and snug gold caps covering their heads. Their short swords were raised high, ready for battle. And, from their vacant stares, they were each quite blind.

Pandy, Alcie, and Iole froze.

But Homer sprang into action.

He dropped the pouches and water-skins where he stood. Reaching up, he tore one of the nearby red silk curtains from its gold rod and threw it over two of the advancing guards. As they were stunned and thrashing about, Homer quickly snatched both of their swords.

And became a gladiator.

All the guards immediately turned on him. Homer, brandishing a sword in each hand and a warrior glint in his eyes, slashed and sliced and ripped and hacked, whirled and dove and ducked and leaped. He inflicted severe damage on the guards without sustaining so much as a scratch. He twisted his body, avoiding a sharp thrust, then twisted again, narrowly escaping a whistling downward pass. Three times he plunged his swords deep, three times a guard fell lifeless.

"How can they see?" Pandy asked Iole.

"I don't know," Iole replied, curtly. "I don't know anything."

"Fine!"

"Fine!"

Pandy rolled her eyes, which caused some pain, and looked back toward the fight in time to see Dido disappear around a corner farther into the chamber.

"Dido," she called feebly, but he was gone.

The last two guards, each missing a limb, were circling Homer, one on either side. In a flash they rushed in. Homer stepped neatly back and watched as they crashed into each other. As the guards stumbled backward, Homer stepped forward again and, arms out to either side, drove both blades home in one swift motion.

Finished, he threw down the swords. He turned toward the girls, but focused his eyes on Alcie and grinned sheepishly.

"It's just what I learned in . . ."

"Gladiator school!" she said, hugging him.

Suddenly, coming from the direction Dido had gone, they heard a woman's voice screaming, then a gurgle, then a snap, then silence.

Homer picked up the swords again and, with Pandy hobbling in the lead, the group made its way deeper into the white marble chamber.

Rounding the corner, they saw two square platforms in the middle of the room with steps on each side. There was an expanse between the two platforms with a large fountain in the center. On top of one of the platforms were two small desks; one held a brush and some small items Pandy couldn't quite make out. The only thing on the other desk was a highly polished metal mirror in a gold frame, held firmly in the hands of a young girl seated on a gold stool. This girl appeared to be no more than ten years old and was covered head to toe in gold and jewels. Her fingers were almost invisible for the number of heavy rings she wore. One ring held a ruby the size of a black olive; another ring bore a light blue stone so big it could have been mistaken for a bird egg. Her toes looked exactly the same, only the stones were smaller and clinked together as she swung her feet. Her forearms were encased in a two long gold bracelets in the shape of writhing serpents, and on her head she wore an oddly shaped, ornate headpiece— made entirely of gold. Only her face was obscured by the mirror. At her feet lay a servant, her head crooked at an unnatural angle, her eyes wide. A comb was still clutched in her hand.

Deeper into the chamber, several women, all blind, clung to each other in fear.

Looking past them, along the walls covered with symbols and stick figures, beyond the pillars shaped like giant palm trees, and into the very corners of the immense room, Pandy understood the reason why the caskets in the palace burial chambers were all empty, as she saw in the vision of the crystal panels.

Hundreds of mummies rested everywhere, leaning in on each other, all propped upright, some fresh, most in decay. They were all dressed as they had been in life: royal robes, gold headdresses and ankle cuffs, and strange symbols of power and authority—a whip of some kind with horsehair and beads, and a crooked staff. More horrifyingly, though, one of the platforms had mummies standing on every step of the side facing the queen; dozens and dozens, forming a human pyramid of the dead. Every mummy in the chamber was positioned so as to face the second platform and Cleopatra.

Without averting her gaze, the young queen turned her head slightly toward her servants and shrieked. Pandy saw the skeletal features; dark circles under eyes that were wild and crazed, high cheekbones plainly visible through her thin skin. One of the women moved up the steps; feeling for the hairbrush. She stood behind the girl and began to brush her long black hair, all the while speaking in soft tones and making delicate cooing sounds.

The girl ignored her, staring only at the mirror. Pandy noticed that, no matter which way the girl turned, some part of her was always touching the mirror; one or both of her hands, sometimes only the tip of her finger as she traced it slowly around the carved frame.

A flash of white brought Pandy's attention to a far wall where Dido stood, surrounded by at least twenty of the most bizarre cats she could imagine. It wasn't the gold and ruby collars they wore: it was the fur. Each cat was glistening and multicolored—she'd only seen that coloring before on a peacock. Dido couldn't move without a cat either hissing or swatting at him.

And then Pandy saw a sightless woman off to one side walking back and forth, over and over between two huge pillars, speaking silently to herself.

"She's counting the steps," Pandy murmured.

On another side of the chamber, two women explored the walls with their fingertips, feeling every nick and bump, identifying each mummy they touched and exactly how it was placed, counting the number of stone blocks that ran the length of the wall, the number of steps required to move from one point to another.

"They need to memorize the entire room," Iole said.

Then a low hum of voices caught everyone's attention.

"Great Zeus! Look," Alcie said in a choked whisper.

Before Cleopatra's platform, four slaves were chained to the floor. They were kneeling on the hard marble, ankles and arms cuffed to short chains that had been anchored to the floor with iron rings. Their heads were placed into narrow rests that were attached to straight iron rods set into the floor; not allowing any movement from side to side and forcing them to look straight and only at Cleopatra.

"I'll just bet *they're* not blind," whispered Alcie.

"Of course," said Pandy. "It makes sense. She has to have somebody to look at her. To tell her how beautiful she is."

"So she chains them up so they can't see anything but her," said Iole.

"That's wrong in so many ways, I can't even think about it," said Alcie.

"Back up," whispered Pandy, slowly retreating back around the corner.

"Pomegranates! What's with all the wrapped bodies?"

asked Alcie, when they had huddled out of Cleopatra's line of sight.

"I think she's unburied everyone who had a tomb in this palace," said Pandy.

"It's more of an audience," said Iole. "And she doesn't have to worry about them stealing the mirror."

"Even the dead have to worship her," said Homer.

"Okay," Pandy said. "Cleopatra must know that Homer defeated her guards, right?"

"Probably," said Homer.

"So why hasn't she sent any more?" asked Iole.

"Because she's crazy?" replied Alcie

"She's not. She's under a spell," said Pandy.

"Maybe she doesn't have any more guards here," said Alcie.

"Wait!" said Pandy. "Maybe she *doesn't* know. Maybe she thinks we're dead and she doesn't need any more."

"Exactly! We bypassed other guards by coming directly into her chamber, but she obviously hasn't seen us," said Iole.

"Right," said Pandy, already withdrawing the adamantine net and the box. "So that means it's her and those women and us. Somehow we have to distract her from the mirror so I can put it into the box. But I can't do that alone . . ."

"Give me the box," said Alcie.

"What?" said Pandy.

"We have to open it while you're holding the mirror. You have to keep Vanity in the net. You don't have four arms, Pandy. Great Hermes' teeth, now you barely have two. So gimme."

"Trust her," said Iole to Pandy.

"Okay," said Pandy, putting the precious, terrible box in Alcie's hands.

"Homer, you get her attention and we'll get the mirror. Think you can do it?" asked Pandy.

Homer thought a moment.

"Yes," he said finally. Then, looking at Alcie, "Forgive me."

"Huh? Why?" she said.

"I'm sorry," he said.

Homer stood and walked to the corner. He closed his eyes, took a deep breath, and strode back into the chamber reciting distinctly and with great emotion the poem he had composed for Alcie's ears alone.

Instantly, there was commotion on the platform, but Homer's voice rang out strong and clear as he paced his steps into the room. He paused only a few times to change certain words for greater effect.

And the effect was swift.

Cleopatra stood up at once, knocking her servant with the hairbrush down off the platform. She listened to his words of praise, but with no smile. Instead, she grew more proud, as if every word from the stranger was, after all, only the honest truth. Clutching the mirror, she stepped over the dead woman at her feet and began walking toward Homer. By this time, Homer had come to the end of the poem. In the silence, a look of rage came over the young queen. Homer began to improvise, pulling words and phrases seemingly out of the very air.

"You are lovelier still than Aphrodite, she of the snow white arms and golden hair," he went on, now moving toward the far side of the room. Backing away from Cleopatra, he accidentally kicked a mummy resting on a pillar, sending it to the floor, the bones inside disintegrating and the wrappings deflating in a puff of dust. Cleopatra was unfazed, concentrating only on Homer.

"She's got the mirror with her!" hissed Alcie.

"I know. I didn't think of that," said Pandy.

By now, Cleopatra had her back to the girls and was completely mesmerized by Homer's every word.

"I'll get it," said Iole. Pandy put out a wrinkled hand, but Iole batted it away. "I'll get it."

Before Pandy or Alcie could protest further, she silently stole out into the chamber. Moving without a sound, she was almost upon Cleopatra when several of the cats surrounding Dido hissed and wailed violently in her direction.

Cleopatra jerked her head sharply, as if the cats had

spoken directly to her. She whirled and picked Iole up by her arm, using only three fingers of her right hand. She gazed into Iole's face, holding her aloft.

"Tell me," she asked, in a high, delicate voice. "Do you think I'm beautiful?"

Iole was too surprised to speak.

Cleopatra shook Iole once and everyone heard the bone of her upper arm crack. Iole fainted.

"Too late." Cleopatra smiled.

CHAPTER TWENTY-FIVE

Battle

11:46 p.m.

Cleopatra dropped Iole as if she were a sack of grain and stared at Homer.

"More," she said, her voice light and incredulous. Behind her, far away, her servants stood confused, unable to find their mistress.

Pandy and Alcie were circling from another angle.

"More!" Cleopatra screamed at Homer.

"You are the sun!" Pandy spoke up, drawing the queen's attention to herself. "Even the sun can't outshine you! You're really . . . bright and . . . big." She was moving slowly around the perimeter of the room, trying to lead Cleopatra away from Iole, who was unconscious on the floor. And she was trying to think fast, but she truly had no idea what she was doing; more important, she had no idea what her body was now capable of doing. "Birds come when you call. Animals will eat out of your hand. Your loveliness is beyond compare." She tried to remember any love poems she'd ever heard. "You are . . . uh . . . heavenly—gold crowned. Perfection. All beauty is in you. Um, perfection . . ."

"You already said that," interrupted Cleopatra.

"You're flawless. You're unique. You're certainly not like me—"

"You? You're old!"

Pandy was dumbfounded for a split second, then she remembered her appearance.

"Yes!" she said. "I'm very old, so . . . I've seen a lot. And you're more beautiful than . . . anyone. Even . . . even Helen and Hippia. They were the most popular girls back in Athens, but you are much prettier—"

"No!" Cleopatra spat, waving the mirror, occasionally gazing at herself. "Not pretty. What is pretty? That's common! Pretty is a sunset . . . or a cat . . . or an emerald. It doesn't mean the same thing!"

"Beautiful!" Pandy said quickly, realizing the truth of what the queen said as Cleopatra moved toward her. "I meant beautiful. You're right. It doesn't mean the same thing at all. I . . . I . . . should have my tongue cut out!"

"I will see to it personally," said Cleopatra, smiling.

Suddenly, Pandy remembered Sigma, the dolphin, and how fast and confusing his speech was at first. Pandy began speaking rapidly, making up words and gibberish sentences.

"Stunning-golden-bee-with-honey-and-beautiful-lovely-moon-no-words-for-your-untamed-gorgiosity-in-the-morning-appreciation-can't-compare-with-flawless-exquisitude-above-excellent," she said, now hopping on her wrinkled, knotted feet and waving her arms. She also tucked the adamantine net into her silver girdle as she pretended to fawn over the queen. Alcie joined in, her two left feet distracting Cleopatra for a second.

Homer used that moment to tackle the girl, trying to knock the mirror out of her hands. He only succeeded in pinning her to the ground for an instant. In a twisted fury, Cleopatra threw Homer off, but he wasn't hurt and tried to seize her again. Again she hurled him away; so hard and fast that he crashed against a far wall, stunned but not unconscious. Still, Cleopatra held fast to the mirror.

Then the queen turned on Pandy.

"Speak of my beauty!" the high voice commanded. "If you do so well enough, Osiris may take pity on your ancient soul when I send it to him. Speak!"

With that, Cleopatra took off at a run after Pandora.

Pandy arced to the right as she retreated, bumping hard into Alcie; so hard that Alcie stumbled backward and flailed her arms, sending the box flying into the nearby wall.

Immediately, Pandy stopped to see what, if anything, had happened to it, but Alcie screamed at her, "Go!"

Alcie threw her body over the box and began to feel underneath her stomach: the box was intact, the clasp was fastened tight, the hairpin was still in place, and the leather strap was secure.

Pandy was hobbling before Cleopatra; the queen was stronger, but Pandy had a good head start and, even at seventy-three, Pandy's legs were much longer so she was outstriding the ten-year-old girl. She used all of her strength to topple several mummies in the queen's path, slowing Cleopatra and giving Pandy time to think. She grabbed the crooked staff from one mummy and used it as a walking stick to quicken her pace. She saw Homer getting to his feet.

She heard a thud and cry. Turning back, she saw Cleopatra's handmaidens rushing around the chamber to find her. One had just stumbled into Cleopatra's path, tripping her and sending her sprawling. Pandy turned just as another servant accidentally dislodged a mummy to Pandy's left, sending it crashing to the floor. Though most of the mummy missed her entirely, her foot was caught for a second. Already out of breath from running, Pandy used precious reserves of strength to free her foot, poking the mummy with the staff and sending up clouds of dust. Turning around, she headed for Homer.

Behind her, she heard Cleopatra alternately pushing the servants away, then commanding them to help her off the floor.

Up ahead, Homer was carrying Iole, still unconscious, to the far side of the room.

Freeing herself from her handmaids, Cleopatra took
off again, but two disoriented servants caused her to fall
into the large, shallow fountain in the middle of the
room where she cracked her head on the tiles. Hard.

Still hobbling, Pandy looked back and saw Cleopatra
floating facedown.

"How's Iole?" she asked, reaching Homer.

"She's breathing," Homer replied.

"What are we doing?" called Alcie from across the
room.

"Stay there for a sec," Pandy answered. "Do you
think she's . . . ?" Pandy asked, indicating Cleopatra.

"Dead? No," said Homer. "She's only ten, but she's
stronger than anyone I've battled."

Pandy looked up at the nearby pyramid of mummies, hit with a sudden idea.

"Homer," she said, "get on top of that platform and
when I tell you, push all of those bodies off the steps
into the center. I'm gonna try to get her—"

"Uh-oh," said Homer.

Pandy turned and saw Cleopatra sitting up and shaking her head. In a flash she was out of the fountain, still
grasping the mirror and searching for Pandy.

"Okay . . . okay," Pandy whispered, taking off again.
"Just listen for me."

She hobbled farther down the length of the room. She passed the circle of multicolored cats; Dido was nowhere to be seen. Pandy allowed herself a second of relief that Dido had somehow escaped and then kept hobbling. Cleopatra spotted her and ran after her, although the heaviness of her water-soaked robes slowed her somewhat.

Homer slumped to the ground and pretended he was still unconscious. After Cleopatra sped by him, he raced onto the platform.

By this time, Pandy had gone around behind the platform and was back where she'd started with Alcie.

"Stay here and when she comes around, tell her where I am," she whispered to Alcie, hobbling into the space between the fountain and the mummy pyramid.

With tremendous effort, Pandy crossed to the other side, where seconds before she'd been talking to Homer.

"Uh . . . here she is!" she heard Alcie shout. Alcie was waving to Cleopatra and pointing at Pandy.

The queen sped around the corner and, spying Pandy across the room, leaped for her.

"Homer, *now*!" she called, her strength almost gone.

Bruised as he was, Homer pushed powerfully against the top few rows of bodies. It was harder than he'd anticipated; though the bodies were mostly dust, he hadn't counted on the tremendous weight of the gold, heavy cloth, and precious jewels.

This, however, was exactly what Pandy had expected. The entire mummy pyramid came tumbling down like a house made entirely out of dried leaves.

The last image Pandy had of Cleopatra was the young queen throwing up her hands, utter shock on her face as sixty mummies, some in full battle dress, some in heavy royal robes, cascaded down upon her head, completely burying her.

But not before an odd-shaped crown caught, as it fell, the corner of her mirror, knocking it loose from her grip and sending it skittering across the floor.

CHAPTER TWENTY-SIX

Vanity
Midnight

"Stay back!" Pandy yelled in Egyptian, hurrying as best she could toward the mirror. "Don't touch it!"

On the smooth marble floor, the mirror had slid easily almost the entire length of the room. It had caromed off a pillar, but was still visible far in the distance. A servant had heard something *whoosh* toward her feet, then stop. Now she was feeling for whatever it was.

"It's her mirror," called Alcie, on the run.

The servant wailed and cringed in horror, moving quickly off in the opposite direction.

As she moved, Pandy saw the gleaming metal surface of the mirror begin to glow. The nearer she got, the brighter it became. Now translucent bubbles the size of apricots were beginning to form on the surface.

"It's got nowhere to go," she said softly.

"What?" said Alcie, reaching her friend and slipping her arm around Pandy's thin waist to help her run.

"It's got nowhere to go. Vanity has nobody to . . . to . . . infect. And . . . we're going to the right!"

"Sorry," said Alcie, trying to correct their course.

"Hurry! They're gonna fly off!" said Pandy, still a good distance away, watching the beautiful iridescent bubbles grow larger. There was almost nothing keeping them attached to the mirror at this point.

"Oranges!"

Alcie thrust the box into Pandy's hands and quickly lifted Pandy into her arms, fighting to stay straight. Pandy didn't say word; she kept her eyes on the mirror. They were only a few steps away when the first bubble broke loose and floated into the air.

"Gods, no! Put me down!" Pandy said. Alcie set her lightly on the ground.

Pandy took the net from her girdle and threw it high into the air, trying to catch the rogue bubble. Her strength gone, she missed it and the bubble of Vanity ascended higher. But the net came down squarely on top on of the mirror, trapping everything, including those bubbles that had just broken free. However, as more and more bubbles formed on the mirror, the force of Vanity now began lifting the net into the air. The rogue bubble was darting and dancing overhead as the others tried to join it.

"Great Athena," said Alcie.

"No," said Pandy, "this is good."

"Huh?"

"Watch," Pandy said, and she started to gather together the bottom of the net as it floated up.

"Don't touch it with your bare hands!" cried Alcie, keeping an eye on the rogue bubble.

"It's just the net."

"Jealousy? It poked through, remember?"

"Right," Pandy said.

She grabbed a fistful of wrapping from the nearest mummy and was binding her hands when Alcie yelled, "It's getting too high!"

The net was being carried aloft; in seconds it would be too high for her to reach. Ever.

"On my shoulders," said Homer, behind them.

Without hesitation, Pandy handed the box back to Alcie and clambered (with a slight shove from Alcie) onto Homer's back, then tried to hobble her way up onto his shoulders. But she was so weak that Homer reached back and, holding her legs steady, simply lifted her into the air.

"Try to stay straight as iron," he said.

"Okay."

Homer maneuvered Pandy directly under the adamantine net and she grabbed the bottom edges only an instant before it would have sailed away. Pinching the edges of the net together tightly, Homer lowered her to the ground.

That was the moment Alcie saw the rogue bubble of Vanity fly into Pandy's wrinkled ear. "Apricots!"

Pandy still held onto the net, but now she twirled it in front of her and began to giggle.

"Look at the lights!" she said brightly. "They're so beautiful. Like me."

"Whoa," said Homer.

Alcie tried to process that her best friend, looking even older than her grandmother, was now infected with a smidgen of Vanity and thought she was stunning.

"Let's let them go!" Pandy said, loosening her grasp on the net.

"No!" said Homer.

"I have a *better* idea!" said Alcie, tapping the box. "Let's put them all in here so you'll always know where they are, in case you ever need one again. Not that you will, because—plums—you're . . . you're . . . amazing!"

"Oh, I like that," Pandy said in a girlish voice. "What do we do?"

"Okay," said Alcie firmly. She undid the leather strap, took the hairpin out of the lock, and unfastened the clasp. "Just lower the net to the floor and open the ends a bit. Good. Now I'll slide the box inside . . . close the net up again, good. Now, when I open the box you just push the little bubbles inside."

"Gently, right?"

"Yeah, gently, whatever."

But when Alcie opened the box, Pandy fussed and clucked, sort of "urging" the bubbles inside. Alcie saw a trail of dark smoke begin to poke its way out from under the lid of the box—Jealousy trying to escape!

"Beat 'em!" Alcie cried. "Push them in!"

Pandy was so startled she instantly began slapping the inflated net with her wrapped hands. As each of the little bubbles was forced into the box (which forced Jealousy back as well), it exploded with a little sigh. Homer grabbed his cloak and began pushing at Vanity as well. Within moments, every last bubble had burst inside and Alcie snapped the lid shut.

She lifted the net off the box (closing the clasp, putting the pin in place, and tightening the strap) and started to put them both in her pouch.

"I'll take the box now," said Pandy.

"I'm gonna hold it for a bit," said Alcie.

"Give me that box!"

Alcie wondered what the tiny bubble of Vanity running around Pandy's brain could do to her. She'd seen the full effect of pure Vanity; Cleopatra had killed, tortured, and maimed so people would revere her. Pandy couldn't be that bad—after all, Vanity wasn't full strength, and Pandy wasn't full strength. But a look suddenly crossed Pandy's face that said Pandy would do whatever she needed to, even to her very best friend, to get the box.

Alcie spied the mirror, now an ordinary piece of shining metal, and quickly picked it up.

"Here," she cried, shoving it into Pandy's hands. "Who's that? Huh? Who's that beautiful girl . . . woman . . . thing? That's you! Look at that!"

"It's me!" Pandy cried, in voice that broke Alcie's heart in two. "Look at me! I've never seen anything so glorious!"

Pandy wandered away, staring at herself.

"Oh, this is not good," Alcie said to Homer, beginning to cry. "This is not good at all."

"No," said a high, cracked voice from behind. "You've got quite the problem, don't you?"

Alcie and Homer spun around to see the orange robes and sharp, pointed smile of Wang Chun Lo.

CHAPTER TWENTY-SEVEN

Wang Chun Lo?

12:11 a.m.

"My, my," Wang Chun Lo said. "What *shall* we do about this?"

"You saw the whole thing, didn't you?" Alcie said, furious at him for some reason she couldn't place. "You knew this would happen!"

"No, Alcestis," he said. "I did not know. And yes, I was watching."

He paused, a kindness in his face.

"I have not seen four people more brave in quite a long time, and I have seen battles that would make you shudder."

"How could you know anything?" Alcie cried. "You're an old man who runs a caravan. You walk through crystals and . . . and you take people's money . . . and you let a girl turn into an old woman! You're worse than my aunt Medusa!"

"Alcie . . . ," said Homer.

Wang Chun Lo merely smiled and thought for a moment.

"Let us attend to the others first, before we decide what is what."

And he moved off into the room toward the towering pile of mummies, disappearing behind a pillar.

"Apples! I'd like to decide a few things, like how to roast an old man," muttered Alcie as she and Homer turned to follow.

They had not taken more than a step when they saw Wang Chun Lo's orange robes lying in a heap on the floor just ahead.

"Well, that's just wonderful," Alcie said. "Now he's naked!"

But as they stared, the robes began to glow white-hot; forming themselves into a ball, lifting into the air, and rushing out the large opening at the end of the room, disappearing into the night.

They saw the ribbon of coins, also lying on the ground, become a large centipede and his long black, braided queue, cut from his head, become a writhing black snake.

Alcie saw Iole first, standing against the wall, cradling her broken arm, her mouth open, staring at something in the middle of the room. Pandy was just beyond her, gazing into the mirror, oblivious to anything else.

Passing the few remaining pillars, Alcie and Homer came to a sudden halt.

Standing close to the pile of mummies was a large man dressed in a simple white robe with a beaded collar, a pointed blue headdress, and light green skin.

With a tiny smile, he waved his hand and at once all of the mummies, including those burying Cleopatra, lifted into the air and began swirling in a huge circle. With a flick of his hand, the man sent the mummies, dust, wrappings, dressings, and jewelry out of the chamber through an entryway at the end of the room.

Watching them go, a question formed in Alcie's mind.

"They will sort themselves out and return each to their own sarcophagus," he answered her. This had to be Wang Chun Lo, she thought, but the voice was now deep and smooth.

"Now," he said, "come to me."

Alcie, Iole, and Homer suddenly found themselves standing before him.

"There is not much time; I shall be brief . . ."

On the floor behind him, Cleopatra, freed from both the curse and her tomb of mummies, began to stir. At once, all attention focused on the queen, now merely a sleepy little girl. She opened her eyes and the first people she spied were Homer, Alcie, and Iole. There was absolutely no sign of recognition and she felt herself grow slightly angry that there were visitors in her private chambers and no one had bothered to help her up. And . . . and . . . why was she on the floor?

Then she looked at the green man and her eyes went wide.

"By all my fathers," she whispered, terrified. "Osiris . . . my lord! I greet you."

As Cleopatra scrambled to kneel, Alcie, Iole, and Homer turned and stared at Osiris, great God of the Egyptian Underworld.

Even Alcie had been paying attention in class back in Athens when Osiris had been discussed as being one of the most powerful gods known to man. He was the Egyptian equivalent of Hades, but the reverence and respect for death and the dead in Egypt gave Osiris almost as much power as Zeus in the minds of his own people. He was, Alcie knew, the only deity that the Egyptians would simply refer to as "God." She thought about the way she'd last spoken to him and waited for the moment he was going to strike her dead.

Osiris threw back his head and laughed.

"I shall not kill you. Indeed that is the farthest thing from my mind. My realms are only for those who have fulfilled their time upon earth and have lived a good and honorable life. Your time is incomplete and you have many honorable deeds yet to accomplish."

He turned to Cleopatra.

"Go to your bedchamber and sleep."

Without a word, Cleopatra stood and walked toward a small entryway at the rear of the room.

"And eat something when you awaken."

Osiris turned back.

"She will, indeed, be the most beautiful of queens. But that will happen naturally. And I know Egypt will be that which she loves most, not her own visage in a piece of metal. What happened here is no fault of her making. She must not be punished. Neither must those whom she has hurt continue to suffer."

He passed his hand around the room, over all of the servants and the slaves shackled to the floor in front of the platform. Instantly, there was a great collective gasp as sight returned to each woman and the chains and iron rings disappeared. There was so much astonished joy, laughter, and confusion that Osiris had to bellow to be heard. At once, all the women and the sighted slaves looked toward the center of the room then dropped to their knees, their faces to the floor.

"We'll just leave them like that for the time being," Osiris said. Then he turned to Iole as if listening to her thoughts.

"My skin is green, inquisitive one, because I rule over the dead. Death is associated with green, rotting flesh." He paused for a second, then smiled.

"I'm sorry you asked too."

"Come, come!" he laughed. "Enough silence! Where

are the chatterers I had in my tent only hours ago? Speak your minds!"

"Why did you pretend to be Wang Chun Lo?" asked Iole.

"I could tell you that it was because I knew you all were coming, and that I needed to be secretive until the curse upon the queen had been lifted."

"But that's not the real reason?" Iole said, rubbing her broken arm gently.

"No, not fully," he said, smiling. "I have been alive since the dawn of time. To be honest, which you deserve, I get bored. Thus, I have frequently roamed my domain in different forms from all over the known and undiscovered worlds. I interact with my people, bringing them new cultures and ideas, thereby hastening the progress of Egypt. Wang Chun Lo did exist, not very long ago. His passing occurred shortly after his caravan entered Egypt. As such, he descended to my underworld and, after telling me his tale, I decided to carry on for a bit in his form . . . one I happen to like very much. I like the caravan and its performers with all of their human flaws. And I love the food."

"Why did you need to be . . . like . . . secretive?" said Homer.

Osiris's face clouded.

"It is in keeping with a pact made with Zeus a short time after Pandora allowed the evils to be freed. I promised I would not proffer aid in capturing Vanity when you arrived in Egypt, which of course, we knew you would—arrive, that is."

"Then why did you help Pandy through the crystal?" Iole asked.

"Right . . . sir," said Alcie. "And why did you let Pandy get old?"

"That was not direct help. Pandora realized the secret on her own due to her cunning and curiosity. She asked and I agreed . . . as Wang Chun Lo. And I didn't simply *let* her, Alcestis. I gave her the option."

"Can you put her back to normal?" Alcie asked, looking past Iole to Pandy, who was still caught up in her own reflection.

"I could. But I cannot," he said somberly. "She made a sacrifice for you and for her quest and she must honor it. What I can do, however, is alleviate the disturbance of Vanity."

"You can put it in the box?" said Alcie.

"No," Osiris said. "As I promised Zeus, I would have nothing whatsoever to do with the box. I shall amend Vanity's effect, however. It shall become the beginning of a healthy sense of self-worth; one that will grow over time into an appreciation, if you will, by Pandora for all of the good things about Pandora. Whatever her age."

Osiris waved his hand. Instantly everyone heard the clatter of the metal mirror as it hit the marble floor.

"What's going on?" Pandy asked, hobbling toward the group, then she gave a start. "Vanity! Where is it? Did I get it? Is it in the box? I got bit on my ear!"

"Iole, if you please," Osiris indicated that Iole should tell the story thus far.

"Osiris, I present Pandora. Pandy-uh . . . or-a, may I present Osiris. He used to be Wang Chun Lo . . ." She rattled off the pertinent points as Pandy stared at the Egyptian god.

". . . and he cannot amend your condition because you struck a deal," she concluded.

In spite of the immense amount of new information, all Pandy could think of was the tea.

"You lied about the tea," she said, not even bothering to address Osiris formally. After all, what did it matter if he killed her? She was seventy-three; she probably had only a few years left at most.

"Not entirely, Pandora," he said with a huge smile. "There are certain Chinese teas with incredible restorative properties. And what I was really telling you is that you must always make time to pause and reflect, let your mind clear every now and then."

Pandy thought it was, very simply, dumb. She wrinkled her brow, but no one could tell.

"Your mother . . . ?" she said, thinking of something else that seemed so unexplainable.

"Yes," said Osiris. "I have one as Wang Chun Lo. She

has no idea that I am not truly her son. I have fortified her natural ability to portend, and I delight in her past greatness. After all, she was once truly the wife of emperors, leader of dynasties. It keeps her happy. And it's nice to finally have a mother. Even her."

Pandy's mind flashed to her own mother. "Even her," she thought.

"Now," he brightened suddenly. "As I have just helped Pandora, I can do something for the three of you. Name a gift and it shall be yours, within reason, mind you. Iole, shall I mend your arm? Homer, you would perhaps wish to be instantly in the house of your father? Alcestis . . . shall I attend to your feet once and for all?"

Alcie's heart jumped. Her feet! She could have her feet back! Her breath started coming in great heaves. She looked from Homer to Iole . . . and then to Pandy. Her best friend, an old woman.

Without warning, an idea hit her square in the heart.

"Iole, Homer," she said, "I need to talk to you privately."

"Alcie, he can hear our thoughts," said Iole, following Homer and Alcie across the room.

"Fine! I don't care. Let's see what he thinks about this."

She revealed her plan, to which there was absolutely no opposition.

"Great Osiris," said Alcie, approaching again and looking him square in the face. "We—all of us—wish that you would restore Pandy . . . Pandora . . . to her original age. Because it is what we wish for, and you made a pact with us, we think that should . . . should . . ."

"*Supersede*," said Iole, softly.

"Supersede, thank you, the pact Pandy made with you. We are all willing to give up our gifts if you do this one thing. Please."

"My arm will heal on its own, great Osiris," Iole said.

"I will see my father when my true destiny allows it, sir," said Homer.

"And I can live with . . . with . . . ," Alcie clenched her jaw and fought back tears, "my feet."

Homer put his arm around Alcie.

Pandy stood there looking at her friends, her heart so full that she thought it would burst. "Of course," she thought, "Osiris wouldn't actually do it, but the very idea that they tried so hard . . ."

"Very well," Osiris said.

"What?" said Alcie.

"What?" said Pandy.

"I said, very well. It shall be done."

"But . . . ," said Alcie.

"Alcestis, you were correct: the sacrifices you three willingly make for your friend do indeed take precedence over her bargain. Pandora would have kept to it,

I know; she herself did not ask for this reversal. I offered you what you wished. And it has nothing to do with Vanity directly, so when next I meet Zeus, I can be truthful and say that I had no direct part in its capture."

He waved his hand.

Pandy felt very hot, then very cold, then for an instant she felt as if she were being stung by a thousand angry hornets. Then it was gone.

She was thirteen, all of her, once again.

CHAPTER TWENTY-EIGHT

A Visit

12:36 a.m.

The skin of her hand was smooth and clear and young: only the same two tiny warts on the fourth knuckle of her right hand were there where they'd always been, which made her giggle.

She ran her tongue over the inside of her mouth. Every tooth was there and she'd never been so happy to have her slight overbite.

She felt her face. Absolutely normal. Her arms and legs, normal. And she began to feel something she never expected: happy with the way she was, warts and all.

Suddenly Alcie was squeezing her so tightly she thought she would faint. Then Iole and Homer came and put their arms around them both.

"Thank you," Pandy whispered over and over.

Pandy broke loose and stepped forward.

"Thank you, great Osiris."

"When I tell you that it was a joy for me, you may

believe it," he said, smiling. "You are all so very, very clever. And I am glad of it. I have not so enjoyed reversing a curse in a long, long time."

Pandy, completely involuntarily, began to cry.

"I am simply not used to this. Such tears," Osiris mused, looking bewildered. "I am used to the wails and lamentations of the dead and their loved ones, but you cry when you should be joyous! Are all Greek maidens so odd?"

"No," said Alcie. "We're special. Pandy, what are you doing?"

Pandy was rooting through her pouch. Digging deep, she withdrew the small vial of her tears.

Uncorking the vial, she held it to her cheeks and chin, catching the precious drops that would operate the map. Hearing Osiris's words, she had begun to feel a little better, so she looked at Alcie's feet and remembered what Alcie had just done for her, and starting crying again.

"Why don't you just use the map now?" Alcie asked.

"Oh, duh!" Pandy said.

"No better time," said Iole.

Pandy looked at Iole's broken arm and, sobbing, quickly got out the blue marble bowl with the three concentric rings and their mysterious symbols. Homer poured a little water into the bowl from his water-skin. Pandy held her finger to her eye, then dipped the tear gently into the water.

Immediately, the rings on the outside of the bowl began spinning left and right, crossing back over each other again and again. As before, two symbols, two distinct words, in a language Pandy recognized as one of the many Berber dialects, finally lined up with each other and radiated the bright blue light.

"Atlas Mountains? Does that mean your uncle, Pandy?" said Alcie, looking at the top ring. "Where's he—or they—or them?"

"Let me show you," said Osiris. He turned toward the wall and began to flick at the air with his finger. Instantly, a map of the Mediterranean Sea appeared showing the islands of Greece, the boot of Italy, the lands of Samaria, Judea, and Syria to the east, and a very narrow strait of water to the far west. Over the city of Alexandria there appeared large blue letters reading "You Are Here." Then a blue line drew itself slowly westward from Alexandria across the top of the African landmass until it stopped on a range of mountains just below the narrow strait.

"Atlas Mountains!" began blinking in bright blue over the mountain range while "Big Rocks!" "End of the Known World!" and "Can't Miss It!" blinked alternately over the range.

Pandy calculated the weeks of travel, even in the swiftest boat. But she knew Hera would be watching the sea; they would have to go by land.

"We'll never make it in time," she said softly.

Iole peered at the bottom ring, anxious to see which evil was to be captured next.

"Laziness!" she cried. "Well, that shouldn't be too perilous. I mean everyone will just be lying around."

"Look at the counter," said Homer.

The counter now read: 157.

Only 157 days left, they all knew, to capture the remaining five evils.

"What's that?" asked Alcie suddenly, looking out the series of large openings that led to the terrace.

Everyone turned to look.

A ball of flame, bright as the sun, was growing larger on the horizon.

"It's too early for dawn," said Iole.

"It's also not big enough to be the sun," said Homer.

"It looks like your orange robe," said Alcie, looking at Osiris.

"It is, in a manner of speaking," he said, smiling.

The bright ball approached fast, forcing everyone except Osiris to shield their eyes. They turned away, their hands tight over their eyes, the glow was so intense. Then, just like that, it stopped.

Pandy turned back, but her eyes needed a few seconds to readjust. When her vision finally cleared, she beheld the beautiful, glowing form.

"Apollo," she whispered.

"Apollo!" Iole gasped, her hand flying to her cheek where Apollo, with only a touch, had cured her illness years before.

"Brother," Apollo said to Osiris.

"Welcome, dear friend," he returned. "You received my message, I see."

"Exactly as planned," Apollo said. "The tiny bit of the sun I gave you to wear was never missed. And having you send it back to me when all had been accomplished was a stroke of sheer genius on my part."

Osiris grinned. "You originally put Vanity in the box, didn't you?"

"Yes. How did you know?"

"A guess."

Apollo glanced around the room. "All is well?"

"It is done," Osiris replied.

"You know, I wanted to be here. To help on a more profound level, but Zeus is keeping an eagle eye on all of us. It's all we can do to distract him."

"You can spare a moment for tea, yes?" asked Osiris.

"From China?"

"You have to ask?"

"Forgive me," said Apollo with a grin, turning his deep blue eyes on Pandy. "Greetings, Pandora."

"Great Apollo," she said softly.

"What did Hermes ask me to say . . . oh yes, your father and brother are fine. They miss you and wish you a speedy return. Or something like that. And your father found his misplaced shell, so call him when you can."

"I will," she said.

"Why the glum faces on the rest of you?" Apollo said, surveying Iole and Alcie.

"They have encountered a problem with the map," Osiris said.

"Problem?"

"Yes, great Sun-God," said Pandy. "We have no way to travel to the Atlas Mountains in time," she paused, a funny sense of familiarity creeping over her. She'd heard of this place before, and not just in geography class. Her father spoke of it as a place forever shrouded in cloudy darkness.

"Perhaps Wang Chun Lo will allow you to cross his crystals again?" Apollo said with a wink to Osiris. By the stricken looks on all their faces, this wasn't particularly funny.

"Right, very well then," he said. "My timing, as usual, couldn't be more perfect."

He held out his hand. In his palm rested a small silver cylinder, about the size of four grains of rice laid end to end.

"Look at it closely, Pandora," Apollo said.

She took the cylinder in her hand. There were tiny holes in both ends.

"It's my whistle."

Pandy looked blank.

"For controlling the steeds of my sun-chariot, you silly thing," he said. "Without this, my horses are too high-spirited for even me to handle, but just one toot on the end of this and they become docile as lambs."

"I don't under—," Pandy said.

"Of course you don't," Apollo said. "That's why I'm explaining it. You see, normally I like to start the sun rising far in the east. But I thought that, just for today, I'd let it rise here. Now, in about twenty minutes, when I'm back on Olympus, Zeus will want to know why the sun isn't coming up in its usual place and I'll tell him that the horses must have gotten loose and since I have misplaced my whistle, it will be very difficult to rein them in. After some mild chastising—blah, blah, blah—he'll send me off to 'get the sun or else!' and I'll just happen to catch it and the horses around . . . let's see . . . the Atlas Mountains. All of which gives you enough time to get into the chariot conveniently waiting outside, toot the whistle, and spend about fifteen minutes congratulating yourselves on pulling the sun across the heavens; something no other humans have ever done."

"Whoa . . . ," murmured Homer.

"Well put, large youth!" said Apollo.

"Thank you, most gracious Apollo," Pandy said.

"It *is* excellent, I know," he said. "Very well, be off with you. Osiris . . . tea?"

"Brother . . . ?" Osiris said.

"What?" said Apollo. Then, as if remembering a trivial detail, "Oh, yes. Don't touch the outside of the chariot or you'll be burned to a cinder."

"Right," said Alcie.

"Thank you," Pandy said. "And thank you, great Osiris."

Pandy, Alcie, and Homer began to collect their things.

Apollo felt a tiny tug on his robe. Looking down, he saw two huge eyes staring up at him.

"Excuse me, wondrous Apollo," Iole whispered.

"Why, Iole," Apollo knelt down, a huge grin on his face, "you're looking quite well, if I do say so myself—and I do, because I did it."

"I just wanted to thank you for . . . my existence."

"Well, normally I *try* not to appear personally in individual cases, scheduling and all that, but your mother prayed most fervently all those years ago. I couldn't resist healing you," Apollo laughed. "And if I hadn't, you wouldn't be doing such a splendid job *and* having such fun!"

He lowered his voice. "I could do your arm, you know, but I don't want to stir up any unnecessary negativity. Don't want to play faves, right?"

"Yes . . . yes," said Iole, hiding her broken arm in her cloak, at a loss for what to say. "I just wanted . . ."

"Me to know how much you appreciate me," Apollo said, rising. "I do."

Then he put his hand on Iole's head, which made her tingly all over.

"You're very welcome, little one," he said.

"Good-bye, Pandora," Osiris was saying, as Iole joined the group. "All good things to you. Good-bye, Iole. Homer. And, Alcie?"

"Yes sir?"

Osiris took a step toward her.

"Always trust that what you do will have its reward. Perhaps not when you want it, but when you least expect it," he said. Then, with a very slight flick of his wrist and a subtle narrowing of his eyes, he pointed them toward the passageway.

"Follow the red line."

CHAPTER TWENTY-NINE

The Way Out

1:27 a.m.

"What did *that* mean? About trust and rewards?" asked Iole, when they had started down the torch-lit passage.

"Who knows?" said Alcie, handing the wooden box and the adamantine net back to Pandy. "Probably just one of those oogly-boogly I'm-such-a-powerful-god things."

"Oogly-boogly?" said Homer, his hand on Alcie's elbow again, guiding her away from the wall.

"Well, I still can't believe you guys did that for me," said Pandy, in the lead. "I was dreading going through the rest of my life looking like Sabina."

"Oogly-boogly?" said Homer.

"Let it go," said Alcie, with a smile over her shoulder.

They had been following a thin red stripe along the wall to their right. They passed silent, darkened entryways, through burial chambers where all the sarcophagi were sealed tightly once again, into and out of several rooms filled with ancient treasures. They passed guards who gave them no trouble, only nods that they should pass. Up and down flights of stairs and through so many anterooms and ante-anterooms they lost count.

All of a sudden, Pandy stopped.

"Iole!"

"What? What's wrong? Did we forget something?"

"How could I be so stupid?"

"What?" said Alcie.

Pandy reached around her neck and unclasped the Eye of Horus. For an instant, she felt the tiniest twinge in her stomach where the pole had pierced her. But that wound was, miraculously, almost healed. And there was no pain at all in her hip or the places where the golden shrapnel had caught her; only a small, golden teardrop scar yet remained under her eye.

Carefully, she brought Iole underneath a torch for better light. Draping the eye over Iole's head, she clasped the pendant again. A look soon came over Iole's face of the sort that Pandy only saw when her father had had a little too much wine or after some of the girls at school snuck off with the youths to eat lotus leaves.

"Good?" asked Pandy.

Iole, very lightly, swung her broken arm from side to side.

"Oh! It's going to be great," she said, hugging Pandy gently with both arms.

"You're not going home . . . right?" Pandy said softly.

"Of course not," Iole whispered.

Onward they went, talking about the adventure that just ended: the black funnel, the dolphins, and the amazing tents of the Caravan of Wonders. Alcie was going on and on about Usumacinta and her birds when Pandy realized that Alcie wasn't behind and to her right, where her feet usually led her. About the same time, Homer realized that he was slowly losing his grasp on Alcie's elbow. Pandy turned around again.

"Alcie, why are you over there?" she asked, walking backward to face her friend.

"What are you talking about? I'm just walking."

"You're walking straight," Pandy said.

"Very funny," Alcie said. "I'm just walking . . ."

Homer plucked a nearby torch from the wall and held it down by Alcie's feet.

There was a left foot . . . and a right foot.

Iole and Pandy both gasped, but Alcie just slumped against the wall, laughing and crying at the same time.

"Osiris. Osiris!" she said, nearly hiccoughing.

A gust of fresh air blew by and they knew that the exit was just ahead.

"Osiris! Oh Gods." Alcie wept, rushing past Pandy right down the very middle of the passageway, a twirl here and a leap there, and out into the desert night. "Oh Gods! OH Gods!"

Pandy, Iole, and Homer quickly joined her, all rejoicing, dancing, and laughing in the half-moon light. Finally Homer spotted the steam rising from Apollo's four snow white stallions, harnessed to a silver and gold chariot.

"We only have minutes. We need to go," he said.

"Right," said Pandy, straightening herself after laughing so hard. "Dido! Come on, boy!"

She paused.

"Where's Dido?" she said, realizing that the last time she'd seen him was in Cleopatra's chamber, surrounded by cats.

"I don't know," said Alcie, still running in circles to the left.

"He's always with you," said Iole. "He has to be around here someplace."

"Dido!" Pandy began yelling. "Ghost dog! Great Zeus—he must have gotten lost. I have to go back!"

"You can't, Pandy," said Iole. "We have to leave right now. Apollo said we couldn't dawdle."

"I can't leave without Dido! It's not dawdling to find my dog!"

All at once a wind picked up, blowing from the south and out over the Mediterranean Sea heading toward Greece. High in the breeze, they each heard a woman's vicious laugh and the sound of barking, yelping, and whimpering.

"Unnnh," Pandy gurgled, unable to find words. Instinctively, she knew exactly whose laugh that was. She clutched her sides and looked at the sky, fearing that the pain in her stomach would kill her. She started for the palace entryway, but she knew it was useless.

"She took him! She's got him!" Pandy wailed, crazed, as the sounds on the wind grew fainter. "Hera's got my dog!"

The steeds of Apollo began to paw the ground with their hooves.

"Homer, help me get her into the chariot," said Alcie, taking charge.

Homer picked up Pandy, now almost incoherent, and, careful not to touch the outside, loaded her into the front. Next Iole, then Alcie, with Homer at the back. Iole wrapped her arms tightly around Pandy as Alcie took the whistle from her hand. With Homer holding tightly to the reins, Alcie blew hard into one end. Immediately, the outside of the chariot glowed a blinding white as it lifted into the fast-fading night sky.

"I'll find you, Dido," Pandy said over and over between sobs, her head limp against Iole's shoulder. Her cries grew louder as the ground fell away. "I promise, ghost dog, I'll get you back . . . wherever you are!"

GLOSSARY

Names, pronunciations, and descriptions of gods, demigods, other integral immortals, places, objects, and fictional personages appearing within these pages. Definitions derived from three primary sources: Edith Hamilton's *Mythology: Timeless Tales of Gods and Heroes*; Webster's Online Dictionary, which derives many of its definitions from Wikipedia, the free encyclopedia (further sources are also indicated on this Web site); and the author's own brain.

Aeolus (AY-o-lus): King of the Winds; a god who lived on earth on a floating island called Aeolia.

Agamemnon (aah-guh-MEM-non): King of Argos who led the Greeks against Troy in the Trojan War.

ambrosia (am-BRO-zee-uh): the food and drink of the gods. Mortals who ate ambrosia became immortal. It is never specified or revealed exactly what it is.

Anubis (uh-NEW-bis): in Egyptian mythology, he is the jackal-headed God of Tombs, whose duty it was to take the souls of the dead before the judge of the infernal regions.

Apollo (uh-POL-oh): God of Music, Poetry, Light, Truth, and the Healing Arts. Often called the "Sun-God," it is Apollo, in his magnificent chariot, who pulls the sun across the heavens each day.

Artemis (AR-teh-miss): twin sister of Apollo; often called the "Lady of Wild Things," and she was huntsman-in-chief of the gods. She was also the protector of youth and young things everywhere; and, commonly, the primary goddess of the moon.

Athena (uh-THEE-nuh): Goddess of Wisdom and Reason. She has no mother, but instead sprang from Zeus's head—fully grown and in full battle dress. She is a fierce warrior-goddess; wily and cunning. She is Zeus's favorite child.

Atlas (AT-lass): one of the original Titans and, in some myths, Prometheus's brother. Zeus condemned Atlas to bear the crushing vault of the heavens on his shoulders forever. (Often he is portrayed as also having to hold up the earth as well, but that's just illogical. I mean, think about it, where would he stand? Hmm?)

caliph (cal-EEF): civil and religious leader of a Muslim state and a successor of Muhammad. One vested with supreme dignity.

calligraphy (cah-LIH-gruh-fee): beautiful handwriting.

Charybdis (kuh-RIB-diss): ship-destroying whirlpool lying on the other side of a narrow strait from Scylla. The myth is that Charybdis stole the oxen of Hercules, was killed by lightning, and changed into the whirlpool.

Cleopatra (klee-oh-PA-tra): (69–30 BC) beautiful and charismatic queen of Egypt; killed herself by allowing a snake to bite her to avoid capture by the Romans.

Crete (KREET): the largest Greek island.

Demeter (de-MEE-ter): sister of Zeus, Goddess of Agriculture and the Harvest; patron of agriculture, planting, crops, health, birth, and marriage.

Hera (HAIR-uh): Zeus's wife and sister. She is the Queen of Heaven and is the protector of marriage, married women, and childbearing. Two words describe Hera: jealous and petty. Of course, that might be because Zeus's many affairs have plagued her since the creation of mythology.

Hermes (HER-mees): the messenger of the gods, the swiftest in action and thought. He was known as "the Master Thief" (having stolen Apollo's herd of cows on the day he was born) and was God of Commerce and the Market, the protector of traders.

Horus (HOR-us): the Egyptian day-god, more specifically he is meant to represent the rising sun. He was son of Osiris and Isis; as an adult he is represented as falcon or hawk headed.

Ionian Sea (eye-OH-nee-an SEE): an arm of the Mediterranean Sea between western Greece and southern Italy.

kohl (COAL): a type of makeup used by women in Egypt and Arabia to darken the edges of their eyelids.

maelstrom (MALE-strum): an enormous whirlpool. A powerful circular current of water (usually the result of conflicting tides).

Notus (NO-tuss): the south wind.

Osiris (oh-SIGH-riss): Egyptian god of the underworld and judge of the dead.

Peking (pay-KING): one of the largest cities in China. Today, it is the capital of the People's Republic of China and is now known as Beijing.

persimmon (per-SIM-uhn): bright orange fruit resembling a large plum or tomato; edible when fully ripe.

Plato (PLAY-toh): ancient Greek philosopher (428–347 BC); pupil of Socrates; teacher of Aristotle.

Poseidon (pos-EYE-don): brother to Zeus and the Lord of the Sea.

Prometheus (pro-MEE-thee-us): a Titan who fought on the side of the gods in the battle for supremacy over the earth and heavens. He also stole fire from Zeus when Zeus refused to share it with mankind. For this he was chained to a rock where a giant eagle would feast on his liver during the day, only to have it grow back at night.

Quetzalcoatl (kwet-zahl-COT-uhl): a primary god of many Mexican and northern Central American civilizations, including the Mayas, Aztecs, and Toltecs. He is represented as a feathered serpent.

queue (KEW, or simply say the letter *q*): a braid of hair at the back of the head.

sarcophagi (sar-COUGH-uh-guy): plural of "sarcophagus." Stone coffins used to entomb mummies.

Scylla (SILLA): a sea nymph transformed into a sea monster who lived on one side of a narrow strait; drowned and devoured sailors who tried to escape Charybdis. In one myth, she is said to have grown dogs' and snakes' heads out of her body. In another, she is depicted with six hideous heads, each mouth with many rows of sharp teeth.

Styx (STICKS): a river in Hades across which Charon carried dead souls.

Yangtze (YANG-t-see): the longest river of Asia; flows eastward from Tibet, through China, and into the East China Sea.

Zeus (ZOOS): the supreme ruler, chief among all the gods, wielder of the mighty lightning bolt (sometimes called thunderbolt). His power is greater than that of all the other gods combined. He is often portrayed as falling in love with one woman after another, which infuriates his wife, Hera.

ACKNOWLEDGMENTS

Thank you to Emily Webster, Richard Overton, Ramona Hennesy, Scott Hennesy, Barbara Rush, William Sterchi, Phyllis Kramer, Karen Smith, Todd McClaren, Nadine Gross, Elizabeth Hailey, and Marcia Wallace.

Special thanks to Nancy Gallt; Harriet Shapiro, PhD; James Kelton; Leah Miller; Michael Scott; Dino Carlaftes; Minnie Schedeen; Elizabeth Schonhorst (who, somehow, makes me happy to edit); my dear "sisters" Josie and Rosie; and, of course, Sarabeth.